Flaming Frontier

Brian Park

A Black Horse Western

ROBERT HALE · LONDON

© 1951, 2003 Gordon Landsborough
This edition 2003

ISBN 0 7090 7337 2

Robert Hale Limited
Clerkenwell House
Clerkenwell Green
London EC1R 0HT

Typeset by
Derek Doyle & Associates, Liverpool.
Printed and bound in Great Britain by
Antony Rowe Limited, Wiltshire

CHAPTER ONE

THE TOMBSTONE FLYER

The line was a pale double ribbon that dissolved into the darkness fifty yards away. Lem Cole had his ear to a rail to catch the first vibrations, and round about eleven he called softly, 'Hyar she comes! Get to yer places!'

Far away came the blue note of the Tombstone Flyer, perceptibly strengthening with each blast. Back in the shadows of some stunted oaks the horses stirred uneasily at the sound.

Lem and his brother Judson went and lay at opposite sides of the track just where the water tank was. Pinky, Irish, and Tucson Tommy went farther back, where they judged the express car would stop. Two minutes after they'd got settled with their guns out, the sweeping beam of the Flyer's headlight came swinging into view, dazzling them as it glared into their eyes. At that they put their faces into the warm Texan earth, so as not to betray themselves with the whiteness of their staring faces.

Brakes screaming, steam hissing, rods clanging, the Tombstone Flyer drew up to take on water. It was still moving as Lem and Jud swung up from opposite sides, and covered a startled driver and fireman.

'What—?' gasped the driver, an old man with a blue, peaked cap and steel-rimmed spectacles. The fire from the box reflected redly on his pursed, toothless mouth and popping eyes behind their glasses.

'Don' talk,' growled Lem, behind his mask. 'Git down!' His heavy Colts punctuated the order with a threatening jerk, and both driver and fireman fell rather than climbed the steel steps down to the track.

'Walk,' now ordered Lem. 'An' no fancy tricks, see!'

'I ain't got no fancy tricks in me, right now,' said the driver firmly. 'Guess I'm the world's best guy at mindin' my own business, pardner. You just say the word; I'll do it!'

A six-shooter in your back and you become suddenly most co-operative. The driver and silent fireman stumbled along the sleepers down the length of the train. Tucson rose out of the darkness. 'Okay?' he whispered hoarsely. 'Everythin's quiet. Guess nobody's taken alarm yet.'

Outside the door of the express car, the hold-up men paused with the prisoners. Lem jabbed his gun into the driver's back. 'Shout to the messenger ter open up,' he ordered. 'He'll know yore voice. An' no tricks, or you'll get yores!'

The driver began to say again that he hadn't no tricks in him, but Lem was impatient and his gun showed it, so the old man let out a shout you could have heard a quarter of a mile away, and that was

6

enough to waken the messenger. He unlocked the door and light streamed out. 'What'n the tarnation?' he began querulously, and then Jud's arm swung and the messenger found his throat gripped as if all vices in hell had got him.

He nearly died of fright in that moment, and Judson found himself having to hold a man whose legs had given out. The big uncouth bandit looked in contempt at the spidery, balding messenger and let him drop, then strode into the car. Lem followed, leaving Tucson standing over the train crew. The plan was working out nicely, smoothly and even to taking over prisoners.

Lem looked at the bags of mail and baskets of parcels. They were no good to him, he knew; the stuff was too bulky. He turned to the small safe that stood back of the car. 'Open it,' he ordered.

'But I can't,' the messenger protested. 'It's my duty—'

Judson jabbed him so hard that he folded up. Lem said, his voice like glacier ice, 'Any more talk o' duty, old timer, an' you'll know what age they'll be puttin' in yore tombstone. Now, git that thar safe open, pronto!'

The messenger got it open, pronto. Lem swore, seeing the contents. A couple of packets, probably containing bonds or securities, neither of which was any use to gun-toting bandits, and a bundle of around five hundred dollars.

'Five hundred dollars,' growled Jud. His eyes looked savagely round to his brother. 'Oughta bin a lot more. Five hundred dollars ain't worth the trouble.'

Then Jud saw the triumph in the messenger's

eyes, the delight at their frustration. That gave Jud one outlet for his temper. His Colt rose, and then the barrel came down and split the bald head down the middle. The messenger looked strangely surprised as the pain rose to envelop him, and then collapsed without a sound, unconscious.

Lem and his brother stood for a moment bathed in the yellow light. Then Jud said, 'I didn't want to hafta do it, but this hyar ain't money enough to satisfy us. Guess we'd better stick up a car.'

This was dangerous work, sticking up a car full of passengers. You didn't know who was reaching down behind someone's back and drawing on you. But the hold-up so far hadn't been profitable, and the gang weren't to be satisfied with peanut money.

Lem leaned out of the coach and fired once into the air. Pinky, Irish and Tommy knew what that meant and immediately opened up with everything they'd got, smashing the windows down the long line of coaches. For three men they sounded like an army, which was the effect intended.

Lem and his brother went down the passage and blew the lock into the first Pullman. As they burst in, they saw the negro attendant running towards them, his eyes rolling with startled fear. Lem sent a couple of shots skimming past his ear, and that turned the negro right round and sent him running into the next coach. Lem let him go. If he started a panic, that negro was as good as ten more men to his gang.

Curtains were part-drawn, and startled faces looked down the aisle. Lem wasn't taking any chances. While Jud crashed over to stand guard at the far door, the gang leader bellowed, 'Get them curtains back, an' all of yer come out where I c'n see yer.'

There was some squealing from the ladies, but they came out, blankets held to their night attire, hair in curlers. The men came too, looking sheepish in their night clothing or part-dressed as some were. Lem's lips curled looking at them. He thought there wasn't a man among the lot; these citified dudes hadn't got no sand or they'd ha' done something.

One man, near to Jud, was thinking the same, though his hands were in the air. 'Two dozen of us,' he thought, 'an' we let two varmints git away with it.' But the thought didn't trouble him; on the contrary there was something like a grin on his face. Like the bandit chief, Tex McQuade didn't think much of these soft town-bred people, and in a vague way he quite enjoyed witnessing their discomfiture. Besides, he was a philosopher. Almost for the first time in his life he was without his guns, and he knew better than to argue with two desperadoes with the drop on him.

A paunchy, indignant little man next to him looked at his big, strong body and whispered, 'You, young man. Do something! Don't let them get away with this!'

'Me?' Tex was amused. 'Why don't you, pardner? You lead, I'll foller.' He grinned, this fat hombre wouldn't do much leading against four loaded guns.

Someone else must have overheard their conversation. That someone was a shapeless form under a blanket, a woman ... a girl, he changed his mind, as she turned towards him.

Tex found himself looking into eyes that were blue as a Mexican sky – but indignant, contemptuous eyes, all the same. Tex saw moist red lips that weren't made for angry words but for pleasanter things – only they were saying, silently, 'Coward!'

Tex pretended to go back in mock amazement. He wasn't bothered about casual opinion, when he couldn't do much else about it except keep his sense of humour. Those hyar people, he guessed, hadn't ever seen how quickly a man can go to Kingdom Come if he ties on to a leaden bullet. Coward? Tex grinned at the thought of it. He was no coward, knew it, and so wasn't bothered by the temporary title.

Jud shouted to them, 'Shut yer mouths; git yer val-ibles an' put 'em in the middle o' the floor.' Lem was getting the case off a pillow and digging through bedding in order to see what had been 'forgotten' there by the owners.

Reluctantly the passengers filed forward and dropped wallets and watches and expensive cigar cases on to a pile near where the watchful Lem stood behind his two guns. Lem said the women could keep their jewellery, as they hadn't time for that this trip, but all the same he took a few pieces that caught his fancy. When they'd all filed past, Jud went swiftly down the beds, searching at his end of the car. He found a few things, then came upon a wallet which had been pushed into a shoe. It seemed well-filled and the train-robber caught the colour of money, so he threw it across to where Lem was packing things into the pillow-case.

Instantly there was something like a scream from the paunchy little man. It was such a shrill, panicky sound that everyone turned to look at him.

Tex saw that the little man's pink, balding head

was deathly white, white with the fear of terrible things. It was midnight, about, and cool, yet the little man was out in a sweat like a mare after a ten-mile gallop. It startled Tex. Losing money was unpleasant, but it wasn't generally a matter of life and death, as the little man appeared to take it now.

'Give me my wallet,' the man screamed. Lem just shoved it into the case. 'I want my wallet! You're not going to have it, you can't take it from me!'

'Keep back!' snarled Lem, behind his mask. 'You ain't got no further need for yore wallet, stranger!'

Tex saw the fat man start to go forward, blind to the danger of the guns in Lem's hands. Tex saw the strained, white, perspiration-wetted face and wondered. Then he caught the significant movement of the bandit's trigger finger, and at once shoved out his foot and sent the paunchy man flying on to one of the beds.

Lem's gun roared, deafening in that confined space. The women screamed, startled, and some of the men swore oaths under their breath – but took care to keep their hands very high.

The paunchy one snapped out of it at that. If he was pale now it was from another emotion – fear of death. He lay where he had fallen, white-faced and trembling, aghast at the thought of his nearness to extinction. Whatever other emotion had driven him before (and it must have been a pretty powerful one), now it was extinguished by thoughts of self-preservation.

Lem's voice rasped through the echoes from the gun blast. 'Don't nobody try no more tricks like that. Guess my finger's itchy, an' it'll be jes' too bad fer the next galoot!'

11

Jud came down the car at that, guns waving menacingly. 'Okay?' he said. Lem nodded. The two backed to the door, slammed it after them and dropped on to the track. They must have been seen by their companions, for immediately the desultory fire on the coaches ceased. Seconds later the passengers heard horses' hooves stampeding away into the darkness – and they knew that that was the end of their money.

At once the Pullman blew up in a bedlam of sound. A couple of women had hysterics, and half a dozen men suddenly found courage and started to say what they'd do to the bandits if only they could lay their hands on them – a pretty safe proceeding, considering that the robbers were at that moment riding too fast to be overtaken by anything short of a swift or Mexican marten.

Tex looked sardonically at the angry mob, then turned to get back to his top berth. To get there he had to pause politely while the paunchy man rose slowly to his feet.

'That,' said Tex calmly, 'was the goldardest silliest thing ter do, pardner. When a guy sticks up a railway train, you c'n bet yer boots he's a pretty des'prit maverick. If you meet up with one o' them guys behind a pair o' guns, don't start doin' anythin' silly. Them guns isn't fer show. They're intended fer use, pardner, so don't give 'em a chance to use 'em. I know what I'm talkin' about, the Border's my old stamping ground.'

He had nearly hoisted himself onto the berth when he felt a hand tugging at his trousers. It was the paunchy man, his face beginning to regain some of its colour.

'I want to talk to you,' he said.

'Okay,' said the Texan, obligingly, descending again. 'What's on yer mind?'

The little man was watching him, a kind of desperate calculation in his stare. Tex felt that he was weighing him up, wondering if he could take a risk. The question that came from the paunchy man, all the same, was startling.

'Ever killed a man?'

Tex's eyes went grey and colourless. That wasn't the question you put to any man, least of all one who had killed – a few times. 'Reckon that ain't none o' yore business,' he said shortly, and turned to climb again. But again that hand restrained him. Now there was a satisfied look in the paunchy man's faded eyes.

'That means you have,' he said softly, pleased. 'Have you got plenty of money? I mean, could you use another thousand dollars?'

Tex gasped, then sat down on the bottom berth. 'Look,' he said, 'you've got somethin' on yore mind. Reckon you'd better spill it, whatever it is. If you're talkin' money, guess I can listen quite easily.'

But the little man was suddenly treading warily, and the big Texan didn't care much for the crafty look that had come into the fellar's eyes.

'You said the Border was yore stamping ground.. Does that mean you can ride, and use a rope, and live hard?'

'Yeah,' drawled Tex, and because he knew it was an important consideration if he were to get into the money stakes, he added what he would have said to few other people— 'An' I c'n use a gun, stranger, use it mighty good. Thar's a few people who could

13

support that statement, only they ain't available.'

'Dead?'

'Ain't livin',' amended Tex agreeably.

The little man was coming to a decision. Tex thought he was making up his mind because there wasn't anything else for him to do.

'If you're free, I'll hire you to undertake a mission, dangerous but well-paid. What's yore business?'

'Cowboy,' returned Tex good-humouredly. 'Got a bit tired of punching cows, an' thought I'd make out at the fight game, so I went North, where the money is.'

'But you didn't make out?'

Tex's eyes greyed as his thoughts flew back to New York, Chicago, Detroit, and a few other towns that had been host to him in the past year. 'Reckon I didn't make out,' he nodded.

No, he hadn't made out. All the time he'd been away his heart had pined for the clean open country that was Texas, the Lone Star State, the State that was alone in the big cowboy's affections.

You could have the big cities, with their lights and colour and fictitious air of excitement. He didn't want any of them any longer. It wasn't that the cities were bad, it was the people in them. To the simple cowboy they seemed like wolves, only wolves infinitely more vicious and dangerous than the ones they got in the New Mexico hills.

But then the city people Tex had come to know were those connected with the fight game, the hardest, crookedest scum in all the cities he'd stayed in. They'd gypped him at every turn. They'd sent him in to fight men with ten times his experience, and for the thrashing he'd taken he'd found himself with the thin end of the cut.

When he began to do better and was able to stand up to the top men, then they'd tried to get him to throw the fight, so that they could clean up on the betting. When he'd refused they got their way by stealth – they always got their way, Tex thought bitterly. Once he'd gone into the ring with a shot of dope inside him that he'd collected via a coffee that his manager had brought specially in to him. He'd been thrashed again, and then the crowd had beaten him up for throwing the fight.

Another time his newest fight manager had tried to turn him, had been refused ... and Tex had been jumped on down a dark passage just before the fight. They hadn't done much to him, deliberately. But you're handicapped if you got into a ring with your knuckles bruised raw from a bare fist fight. That was the last fight Tex lost. Then he decided that the dirt and slime of professional fighting wasn't for him.

One morning Tex had wakened under a grey Detroit sky, stinking as it always did from the giant glue factory down where the bridge crossed into Canada. In his heart was a longing for the wide open prairie, for the warmth of the Texan sun, the blue of its skies and the chivalry and straightness of the men who made the south-west.

Tex went almost straight to the railway station. Almost. He called on his crooked fight manager. That was one fight the manager was engaged in from which he drew no percentage. Tex took the first train out, because some broken-nosed hoodlums could have been on to him if he'd waited for the noon train.

Now, still with a bit of jack heeled away, he was

coming back to take up where he had left off. So, when this li'l runt started talkin' money, why, that was mighty interesting.

As an unsuccessful fighter, Tex was still good material in the fat man's eyes. He was a fighter, a tough man, a man who knew Texas and had killed. That was exactly the man he wanted, even if he hadn't been world heavyweight champion.

'You can take on this job, then?' asked the man eagerly.

'Ain't got nothin' else in mind right now,' drawled the Texan. 'Who d'yer want killin'?' he asked sardonically.

'Nobody. Well, not unless they invite it.'

'Come clean.' Tex was getting impatient. He wanted to get nearer to that money. 'Ante up, an' let's see the face o' yer cards.'

'I'll give you a thousand dollars if you'll get that wallet back for me,' said the little man, and then he strained forward anxiously, as if his life depended on the cowboy's answer.

CHAPTER TWO

LAVENDER GREY

'Wallet? The one them hombres got away with?' Startled, Tex looked round the crowded coach, with its tearful, maudlin, almost-hysterical passengers. The attendant was trying to get them into their berths, but they were reluctant to go. At that moment the train shuddered and jerked, throwing some of them on to the ground, and then they were away again, beginning to pick up speed towards Tombstone and the west-Border towns.

'Yes.' The little man looked quickly around, then talked urgently into his ear. 'Look, cowboy, I've just got to get that wallet back.'

'Money?'

'Not much. Some – er, documents.' The paunchy man went uneasily over the word. Tex knew that if he wasn't lying he wasn't keeping altogether near to the truth. 'You haven't got to know what's in that wallet, and you haven't to look inside, understood?' The little man glared threateningly, as if trying now to frighten Tex from taking a peep in the unlikely

17

event of him ever laying hands on the missing wallet.

'Okay,' soothed Tex. 'Keep yer shirt on, pardner. You want that wallet back, an' you don't want the contents looked at. Okay, I get yer. But what about the thousand dollars?'

That part the little man was cautious about. After a bit of considering, though, he said, 'I'll give you a money order for five hundred now. If you bring me that wallet with the papers intact – I'm not bothered about the money, understand? – I'll make your reward up to a thousand dollars. Do you think you can get me the – papers?'

The little man hung on to his answer. Tex drawled confidently, 'Reckon I might at that. A thousand dollars is a mighty powerful stimulant. I'll take on the job. Now, make out that money order, I'm a-goin' to drop off at the next halt.'

Tex dressed like lightning. The blood was coursing through his veins like a stream of fire. Good old Texas! Things sure happened down here! Five hundred dollars – that was a mighty good start to the prodigal's return and better pay than he'd got in the fight game. And the job – tracking the train robbers – why, durn it, that was a job after his own heart, anyway!

As Tex finished he saw the girl climbing into her berth. He grabbed his grip, looked carefully at the money order that the paunchy man had made out, and prepared to go. But he paused, turning. That name on the order – it read 'Claude C. Hooker.' Now, that was a very familiar name.

'Claude C. Hooker?' he queried slowly. 'Now, where've I heerd yore name afore?'

For once Claude C. Hooker didn't seem so keen on telling him. Then it came out, a bit gruffly, shortly, 'I'm a senator of the United States,' and at that Tex's eyes went wide. He'd heard of Senator Hooker. A bit of a grafter, by all accounts. Tex thought that all politicians must be like fight managers, lousy no-goods that would be better strung to a cottonwood back where their corpses wouldn't offend with their stink.

Tex had learned quite a bit while he was in the East, and what he'd learned wasn't just about the fight game. He'd learned that city politicians were just so many varmints, as he put it himself.

Still, a thousand dollars was money, and he could do with some jack, at any rate in that quantity. He took the order, folded it and put it into his shirt pocket. 'That cash along the Border towns?' he queried.

'At any Brandt & Sius Bank,' said the senator.

'I'll try it at the next halt,' nodded Tex. 'Now, where do I find you, when I get the wallet – or if I don't?'

'Lozier. You'll get me at the Mexicana Hotel. I'll be there a couple of weeks.'

'You'll hear from me before then,' said Tex, but he was thinking, 'Lozier. That's on the Pecos river, plumb on the Mexican Border. It ain't healthy right now, not after the war with Mexico, and senators don't usually put themselves in the firin' line.'

But he said nothing of his thoughts, only stooped and picked his soft-sack grip and went with an abrupt 'So long,' to the senator. There was a lot he didn't like about the politician, a lot he felt he'd like to know about his new boss.

Outside the girl's berth he paused, then rapped gently on the curtain. The girl's enquiring face appeared. It frowned when she saw him. 'Well?'

'Ma'am,' said Tex politely, 'I reckon this hyar train ridin' ain't healthy. I'm a-gittin, off at the next stop. Reckon you c'd come with me, if you'd a mind to.'

The girl just glared and slammed the curtain shut against him, so Tex turned sorrowfully away, shaking his head. 'Reckon I don't even rate so high with that hyar gal,' he told himself, but if his face was solemn, the cheerful Texan was smiling inside. She was a pretty girl, but he didn't get het up about things on account of that.

The car attendant said they would be stopping in a few moments at Carved Buttes, where they'd be able to telegraph the news of the daring train hold-up all along the line. Tex saw that for a negro the attendant looked a mighty pale man, and then found out why.

'Dat messenger, sah, back in the express car. He done die from a bang on the head.' The negro's eyes rolled expressively. 'Ah'm jes' thinkin' it c'd eas'ly have bin me, sah.'

'It sure might,' agreed Tex. 'Lucky fer you, you could run faster'n a bullet.'

'Did I do that?' asked the negro in amazement.

'Sure did,' said Tex. 'Guess you shot back outa that car faster'n the bullet could ketch up with you so the gunman called it back. Guess he val'ied his bullets an' didn't reckon to waste none.'

Carved Buttes was reached, a dimly-lit station on the edge of the desert, asleep when they arrived, because the Tombstone Flyer wasn't scheduled to stop there. One minute the station lay drugged in slumber, only the thousands of flies and skeeters banging against the lamp glasses disturbed the silence, the next it was alive with railway officials, the sheriff and an assistant, the local commandant of a U.S. cavalry company, and the inevitable bums and loafers that spring out of nowhere when there's a free show of any sort.

Tex thought that someone might start to question him, getting off so soon after the robbery, so he went quietly into the shadows and left the station by a door which shouldn't have been open.

Carved Buttes didn't look much of a town, but Tex guessed it would have an hotel, and after a few minutes' blundering in the dark he found it.

The night porter was surly and suspicious and understood even less when he said he had just come in on the Tombstone Flyer. He wanted to argue that that was impossible; the Tombstone Flyer didn't never stop there. But Tex wasn't going to argue with anyone. He just said, 'Wanta say I'm a liar, Big Lugs?'

The porter resented the allusion to his over-size ears, but decided to say nothing when he saw the weight of the Texan's paw, carelessly held roughly two inches from his chin – and clenched nastily. The porter suddenly pulled himself together and said, 'God forbid,' and reached for a room key. 'What time d'yer wanta git up, sir?' he asked.

'First light,' Tex told him, and just over three hours later the big cowboy was out of bed again, seemingly as refreshed as if he had had a full night's unbroken sleep.

His first job was to get a horse. The best he could find wasn't so good, but if it hadn't speed at least it

21

looked as if it would last all day. He got it cheaper than he'd expected, and bought a good set of horse furniture because that was cheap, too. Maybe that was because he was up so early that the liveryman hadn't got the sleep out of his eyes.

Tex loped all the way back to the water tank where the stick-up had been the night before. If he was to trail the bandits, the only way he could think of to get on their track was by riding out to where he could pick up their trail. He was hours late, but there was nothing else for it.

The tank was about an hour's easy riding back up the line, at a place where a perpetual spring kept it always full. There were no houses, no buildings of any kind nearer than Carved Buttes, leastways not the way he had come and he didn't expect there'd be any the other way, where the ground was scrub and rocky and useless for anything.

At the tank there was a confusion of tracks, but they seemed to radiate from or return to a clump of oaks that had to fight hard to live in spite of the plentiful water supply. A trail appeared to come in from the direction of Carved Buttes, and another set led away south across the bare desert. Tex worked it all out, his sharp eyes scanning the tell-tale signs.

A body of horsemen had come in recently from the direction of Carved Buttes. They had halted for quite a long time, had dismounted and left their horses. That would be when they went to shoot up the train. Then they'd returned and ridden of towards the Border, and with them they would have taken Senator Hooker's wallet and papers.

Tex wondered again what could be in those papers to make them so valuable to the senator, wondered especially when he remembered the panic in the man's face when he saw the wallet being taken away.

'Reckon that's some powerful medicine in that hyar wallet,' he thought. 'Mebbe bad medicine. Wal, it ain't none o' my business ter know what's in them papers. All I know is I got five hundred bucks ter follow them bandits, an' thar's another five hundred a-waitin' me if I bring back them papers. Reckon that other five hundred bucks is my business.'

Some distant movement caught his eye. He looked back far down the trail into Carved Buttes. There was a cloud of dust three or four miles back, which betokened a considerable force of horsemen approaching. 'Guess they'll be the sheriff an' some posse a-comin' ter try and find the trail. Reckon I got up a-fore them this morning.'

Tex was trying to work this one out. When bad men stick up a train, they don't go straight to their hide-out; they're inclined to strike off in some other direction, then branch aside where hard ground promises to leave no tracks to betray them. This open trail leading south towards the Border didn't deceive Tex, and he knew it wouldn't deceive the sheriff.

To start with, Tex had seen the bandits, at least above their masks, and he knew they weren't Mexicans. If they were, then Mexico had suddenly found a way of whelping blue-eyed offspring from an essentially brown-eyed race. And with the war with Mexico so recent, Tex knew that even lawless men wouldn't find it safe to cross the frontier, unless they were native Mexicans.

'Guess that's a blind, pointin' towards the Border,'

he ruminated. 'Guess they won't cross the Border but will strike off somewhere this side.'

But where? Would they branch east or west? Tex took a gamble on it. He thought that with Carved Buttes so near, relatively, they'd keep clear of that sector of the country; if that were so, they must be heading down the Border, travelling all the time to meet the sun.

Tex walked his pony down the steeper track for a while. That was so his tracks wouldn't confuse the posse behind – he didn't know what the sheriff would do, but he didn't want to find a posse innocently trailing him for a train bandit – and mebbe shooting it out before he had a chance to explain.

Half a mile down the track he turned south-east and sent his pony loping steadily through the tall cactus and prickly pears. If they'd gone south and then turned east short of the Border, this course of his should eventually bisect their tracks. If he could recognise them, then he'd have saved so much time and would be that much closer on to their trail. If his hunch was wrong, then he'd have to go all the way back and try the other direction, or find the sheriff and see what he'd found.

Either way meant delay, with the trail growing cold. Tex hoped that his hunch would pan out.

He was looking for five tracks – five men had been concerned in that hold-up the night before. 'Only five,' he found himself grinning. They'd made it sound like fifty-five. They'd got guts, those fellows. It takes sand to stick up a train containing several hundred folk and do it with only ten guns. True, the Dalton brothers – just the pair – had stuck up trains successfully, and one hombre had tried to do it single-handed at Cisco some years back and hadn't done too badly, but it was still a daring performance to do it with such a small party.

Tex kept to the soft going all the way. If he came upon a rocky outcrop he would skirt it, holding to the softer ground until he could strike south-east again. There was no sense in crossing hard ground, because if the bandits had happened to cross that same point he'd never see their trail.

Horse and rider plodded on through the alkali, while the sun blistered their necks and sent shimmering waves of heat rising from the nearly white sand of the desert. There was no sign of life, except for an occasional circling buzzard that departed when it saw they were alive and moving. Nothing to see except mile after mile of scrub desert, in patches fantastically decorated with the spiky hands of contorted twisting cactus that grew to heights far taller than a man – cactus that could live a year on the faint dew that was precipitated on occasional nights, live and seem to flourish.

Cactus, prickly pear, and scrub thorn – then desert sand ... mile after mile, unwanted by man or beast, a death trap for the weak and unwary, a nightmare for those who lost their way.

And Tex enjoyed it. After the strident, closed-in life of New York, the hammering, pulsing existence of industrial Cleveland, Pittsburgh and Detroit, this was living again. Space, that's what he wanted all the time he'd been out of the saddle, he now realised. Space to ride and look at and think in. To hell if there was a great ball of sun to make things hot; that didn't count much anyway, if you were used to it. This was the land he knew, this was the country he had known most of his life. Maybe he hadn't exactly been in these parts before, but it was home to him.

They stopped for eats when they found a water cactus unexpectedly. You don't find many of these, otherwise the desert wouldn't be so terrible to travellers. Tex cut it open and got a couple of pints from it before it ran dry; it was cooler than the water in his bottle, so he gave his horse his bottle water and drank from the gourd instead.

There was no time for making coffee; just a rest for the horse, a drink, and then they went on.

Twice they crossed cattle trails, and from the look of them Tex guessed that they were beasts that were being rustled over the Border. It seemed that the Mexicans were busy again, now that the truce had been declared.

Late that afternoon Tex came across what he was looking for. Two horsemen had ridden this way little more than a few hours before; they were heading east, which was as he had hoped and expected.

But – two. Tex shoved back his hat and squinted into the distance as if that way he would find inspiration. Five bandits had started out; were these the tracks of two of them? Tex reckoned they might be. Maybe they hadn't a hideout, but had sought protection by dispersing to different places along the Border.

He took a gamble on it that these were the tracks of two of the men he wanted, and sent his horse plodding after them. There wasn't much doubt where they were going; within half an hour they came in sight of a mud-walled Border town named Destiny. Tex rode in confident that he would find his two men there.

It was a typical frontier town, small, smelly and faded. Unlike the cow-towns farther north, Destiny had few frame buildings, for timber was scarce and expensive so far from the railhead. Instead thick walls of dried stone-hard mud supported Mexican-styled tile-roofs; it was a town of shady courtyards and cool-looking shady balconies, but the architecture didn't bear close scrutiny, and the filth and the flies destroyed any illusion of comfort that the shade suggested, once you stopped.

It was nothing new to Tex. He'd been from one town to another along this Border, even into Destiny on occasions before. He'd got used to them and didn't seem to notice the offence they gave to his skin and nostrils.

There was a branch of the Brandt & Sius Bank close by the ford, he knew, and he turned that way first thing on entering the town. Buying that horse and trappings had cleaned him out, and anyway he felt it would be good to feel some of Hooker's money in his hands. Hooker's signature carried weight even in this remote Border town, and the bank manager had no hesitation in handing over five hundred dollars.

That made Tex feel better, and he rode on in a pleasant state of mind to try and earn the next five hundred.

As he came down the dusty main street, his eyes watched for signs of jaded horseflesh, but none was tethered at any of the hitching rails outside the stores and saloons. So Tex halted by a veranda where a spare old man sat whittling away at a stick.

'Whar's the hotel, old timer?' he drawled. 'I kinda forgot.'

'Hotel? Y'mean ter sleep?' The old timer squirted tobacco juice expertly through the veranda railings. 'Reckon you'll be wantin' Milano Joe's. Ain't what y'd call an hotel, though, stranger. I'm a-warnin' yer. Roun' hyar it's known as a boardin' house. You'll find it where that chestnut stands, 'longside a vacant lot.'

'Thanks, pard,' said Tex, and pulled his tired horse round. The old-timer called, 'Them fleas'll bite the hide off'n you, cowboy. You watch out, I'm a-tellin' you.'

Tex grinned and thought, 'If I've only got fleas to worry about, that five hundred's as good as in my pocket.'

When Tex rode round to Milano Joe's stables, he found two very tired horses there and guessed they were the ones he had been trailing. Well, so far so good.

Milano Joe, voluble and Italian for all his twenty years in America, said sure, there'd be some grub rustled pronto, sure there was a bed for him. 'Jes' sign the register,' he said, and produced a taggy book and scratchy pen. 'We gotta do things proper since the war, signor,' he explained.

Tex looked at the two previous signatures, scarcely decipherable. After a while he decided that one was 'Smith' and the other 'Smithson'. 'Two guys with a sense of humour,' he thought, for not for a moment did he believe those to be the names of the men he had followed.

Tex ate alone in a fly-ridden dining-room, then went and lay on his bed and considered his next move. If these were his men, what next? He decided that the best thing was first, to get his peepers on to the men and see if that told him anything; next, to get into their room, if they would only go out, and see what he might learn there.

From the book it seemed that only he and the Smith-Smithsons were guests at Milano Joe's boarding house, so that when he heard heavy feet on the passage outside, shortly after sunset, he made a guess that it would be his men.

He leaned out of the window, set wide to catch any comforting breeze, and saw two heavily-built men go down the sidewalk and turn into the saloon, already wakening and strumming up for the night. Tex watched narrowly and thought he detected the little signs that show when men are on the run – the tight way they seemed to walk, as if bunched within themselves, as if ready at any moment to go streaking into their gun holsters; the quick way they looked at people as they passed. If they weren't his men, then they were of similar kin.

He went on to the passage and tried a few doors. It was easy to spot the men's – unlocked doors meant empty bedrooms, and only one room was locked against him.

Tex got in easily. He tried the key of his own door and it fitted. That's the sort of establishment that Milano Joe ran.

Inside, the cowboy found there wasn't much to see. Just one waterproof saddlebag containing some spare clothing, that was all. If these men were concerned in the train robbery, then they must have dumped the bulkier loot they'd carried away in the pillowcase, or else the other three had taken it with them.

Or else, he thought again, they weren't his men at all.

He'd searched pretty carefully and was about to leave when he felt something hard wrapped in the folds of a shirt that was in the bag. It was damp to his touch, and Tex guessed it was probably the shirt that one of the men had been wearing earlier that day.

Swiftly he withdrew the object. It was a locket, with a thin gold chain, the kind that women wear. It was an unusual thing to find in a man's sweaty shirt, and Tex opened it.

He found himself looking at a photograph of the girl ... the girl who'd called him coward back on the train.

After a moment the cowboy recognised that it wasn't the girl, couldn't be. The photograph was too old for that, and the dress too old-fashioned. Tex decided that it must be a picture of the girl's mother, but the resemblance was quite remarkable.

Holding it to the light he read the faded ink writing – 'To darling Lavender Grey, from her loving mother.'

Lavender Grey. Now that was a nice name. He stood and looked at the picture. 'She's probably dead, her mother,' he thought and felt sorry for the girl. Probably she was heartbroken, right now, having lost this treasured possession.

He slipped it into his pocket, and turned to go. Anyway, it settled one thing for him – now he had no doubt that these men had been concerned in last night's train hold-up. He went down to the saloon, wondering how to get from these men the knowledge of the whereabouts of those papers that Senator Hooker wanted so badly – and wondered again what they could contain that made them so important to the paunchy little man.

It seemed safe enough, going into the saloon. It was highly unlikely that they would remember his face, seen in the uncertain yellow light of that crowded Pulman.

What Tex wanted to make sure was that he saw their faces now, so that if he lost their trail he would be able to recognise them at a later date. So far he had only seen their backs.

The saloon was hotting up. All day these men of Destiny had worked out in the parching, blinding sun, and now, with the cool of evening, they came and drank like dessicated sponges.

The bar was wet where the foaming glasses came sliding down; there was gambling at a dozen tables; in one corner a cracked piano and a guitar knocked out some Mexican melody with a plaintive chorus in which the near-drunks joined. Some women had appeared, too; one or two half-breeds, with the high cheekbones and brown eyes of their Mexican parent predominant, an Indian girl who'd been stranded in Destiny by some tiring amorist of a cowpuncher, and a faded blonde who said she'd come from Boston but Tex put it no higher than the Bronx.

She came to the table where he had seated himself; he wasn't interested in her, but she was a good cover so he bought her a drink. He thought he wouldn't look so conspicuous, drinking with the girl; it is solitary men who attract attention from gun-toters.

The blonde kept up some conversation that was dreary to listen to and not important anyway, but it was the kind that could be answered without much thinking about, and that suited the fighting cowboy. Under cover of it he looked for the men.

They weren't hard to spot. By a process of elimination it boiled down to two tough hombres who sat near to an open window that gave out on to the broad, cool veranda. Watching them covertly Tex knew that they were mavericks; they had the rogue look about them, the hard, slanting glances of those who find themselves so often in a desperate condition that at all times they are ready for the unexpected – and the worst.

He felt that though they seemed relaxed over their drink, yet their guns would be streaking into flame at the least provocation or sign of danger. And he thought, 'This is gonna be tough. Them guys is sure hard eggs. How the heck am I gonna crack 'em and find out what's inside?'

He decided that the best thing for him was to sit and wait – wait for them to make a move and then keep trailing them until they returned to wherever the loot was.

Someone bent over him. Tex didn't like the breath. It was Milano Joe, all grease and smiles. 'Ah, signor,' he beamed 'Haf you seen Signor Smeeth?'

'Why, sure,' said Tex readily enough. 'There—'

He stopped abruptly. Some suspicion came to him just then but perhaps it was too late. Mebbe he should have pretended that he didn't know Signor Smeeth; after all, why should the Italian boarding-house keeper think he knew them?

Tex tried to cover himself, but it was a bit awkward. 'That the fellar you mean, Joe? Them at the boardin' house like me?'

Joe became voluble, and even greasier, sweating

under the hot yellow lights. 'But I thought you knew them, signor? Are they not friends of the signor?'

'Nope; never seen 'em afore today in my life. Jes' caught a glimpse of 'em leavin' yore place a short time ago.'

Joe thanked him and went across to where the men were drinking. Tex felt somehow uneasy; somehow he'd felt that there was something behind the boarding-house keeper's words.

The blonde was talking again. God knows what she kept on about. But while pretending to talk to her, Tex watched Joe and the two men in conversation together. He couldn't see the men's faces, because they kept them down, but Tex had a feeling that what Joe was telling them didn't please them any.

A couple of minutes later Joe went out and with him went one of the men. The other stayed, ordering a fresh round of drinks as if expecting his companion back shortly. No more than five minutes later the other hombre was back. He said something, at which both men downed their drinks and went quickly out into the darkness.

The blonde continued to talk, and it wasn't till half a minute later that she realised she was talking to herself. Tex had risen, the moment the two hombres went out, and quickly followed.

And right on the last word that the blonde spoke before discovering his desertion from her company, Tex went stone cold unconscious.

For the moment he stepped out into the darkness something mighty hard clubbed on to his skull — hard enough to put him out for the better part of half an hour, anyway.

CHAPTER THREE

IRISH MULLOY

Tex came to consciousness, suddenly but painfully. He found himself slung down across a horse, feet and hands tied together under its belly. That's not the most comfortable way to ride at any time, but when your head's going in and out like a concertina that's being played over a fire, then it's almighty hell. He was gagged, too, so that he couldn't let his captors know he was conscious again, and therefore capable of riding a horse as nature meant them to be ridden.

His eyes told him it was still night, and in time he guessed that he was slung across his own horse. Even in this discomfort he began to put two and two together ...

About a couple of hours later they stopped, and Tex heard a growling voice say, 'Reckon that's safe enough, if thar's any more a-tailin' us.'

'What about this galoot?' That was another voice, no less encouraging.

'He can lie in the sand,' replied the first *hombre*,

34

and Tex didn't think the future looked so good to him.

They just shoved him off the saddle and let him lie where he dropped; they appeared to hobble the horses so as to keep them close, and rolled up in blankets somewhere back of him, and went off almost immediately into sleep. Tex thought they must feel confident in their safety, to go to sleep like that. Tied up as he was, he didn't see much sleep ahead for him – the bonds restricted his circulation, and by early morning his feet and hands felt as if they were dropping off.

With dawn, Tex rolled over so as to have a look at the faces of his captors. One look was sufficient. Messrs. Smith and Smithson lay in the blankets behind him.

Not long afterwards both woke and sat up. Silently they boiled coffee and ate some brown Mexican loaf bread. They gave none to Tex, and didn't even seem to look at him until they'd finished. Then they slung him across the saddle once again and started to ride deeper into the desert.

That wasn't the best of rides that Tex could remember. After a while the blood seemed to get into his aching head to such an extent that he probably passed out once or twice; but even so it was the longest morning's ride ever for Tex. At noon they entered a canyon that was made where a cleft split a high rock outcrop from end to end. It wasn't long, but it was high enough to cast a shadow, and that was something. After they'd thrown Tex off his horse again, he saw that there was water and guessed that this was some secret hideout of the gang. Probably splitting up and going round by way of Destiny was only one way of shaking interfering sheriffs off the trail; probably all the time the idea had been to rendezvous in this place.

If that were so, thought Tex hopefully, then mebbe one of the hombres would come riding in with the missing papers. Then his heart slumped. What good would that do him? He'd be lucky if he came out of this with a whole skin, much less someone else's papers. That next five hundred dollars didn't look nearly so inviting now.

This time, perhaps feeling completely safe, they gave some attention to Tex. One bent and tore the gag out of his mouth and made him sit up.

'Now, yer *hombre*, how 'bout a li'l explainin'?' he growled. 'Who air yer? What's yore name? What're tailin' us for?'

Tex said, 'Fer God's sake, gimme a drink!' His voice was such a croak that he could hardly recognise it.

'Give him nothin', Lem,' said the other man brutally. 'Leave him an' let's get some chow. Thirst'll make him open up later.'

With that he turned and made a small fire, while Lem went to a cache in the rocks and dragged out a sack containing food. It was deliberate torture; when the smell of fried beans and bacon and the wafting odour of coffee was too much for him, Tex decided to talk.

After all, why not? His story was reasonable, or as likely to be reasonable as any he could think of. Somehow he managed to raise his voice into an audible croak. He was pretty far gone, not having tasted anything wet for close on eighteen hours, with the last six hours being spent under the desert sun.

'I'll tell you everythin',' he gasped through cracked lips. 'Only, fer God's sake, water!'

'I ain't in no hurry,' growled Jud. 'We got all the time in the world, hyar. Reckon the longer he waits, Lem, the more likely it'll be the truth when it comes.'

Lem said, 'Guess yore right, Jud,' and shovelled a knifeful of steaming beans into his face.

Tex said, 'Gimme a gun, or let me face yer fist ter fist,' an' I'd see yer in hell afore I'd tell yer anythin'. But like this, wal, I reckon there ain't no harm in keeping it as true as mebbe.'

Jud got up, squinting against the bright light. He wiped his bacon-greasy hands on his soiled pants and then came across and stood over the cowboy. Before Tex realised what was happening, the scrub-faced desperado had him hoisted on to his feet.

'Reckon yer might think we're kiddin', when we say we want the truth outen yer,' said Jud, while Lem watched and gulped his hot coffee from the can. 'So – jes' see we're in arnest.'

Tex saw the thick arm bend back; he was tied tighter than a mummy and couldn't escape it. The big fist came travelling round in a bone-splitting hook plumb into his face. Tex crashed back on to the sand, the world rocking in a red mist of blinding, bloody pain.

Jud had him on his bound legs again before his head had cleared, so that he hardly knew what Jud was saying, hardly saw the next powerful blow that drove into him ... and couldn't have escaped if he'd tried.

'Mebbe we're not so interested in anythin' yore likely ter tell us,' went on Jud in his low, gravelly growl. 'Mebbe it don't matter whether yer speak the truth or yer don't. Jes' larn a lesson now – ter keep yer blasted nose out'n other people's business!'

This time his fist came smashing plumb in the middle, just where the ribs come together – only he hit just where they weren't. It's called the solar plexus, or the diaphragm, and it's a mighty powerful nerve centre. Get a direct blow there and parts of your body go paralysed for minutes on end, and all the time the tortured nerves scream out with the pain they're enduring. Generally you vomit, only Tex couldn't be sick because there was nothing in him to fetch up.

Jud lifted him twice again and smacked him down. Tex didn't say anything, though he wasn't gagged, and he could have spoken because his mouth was no longer dry – there was blood in it, plenty blood. He didn't say anything because he wasn't going to give this blasted, train-robbin', brutal coyote the satisfaction that a squeal would bring.

Then Lem took a hand. 'Aw, Jud, take it steady,' he growled, emptying the coffee can into the sand. 'Reckon that ain't no way ter carry on.'

Tex thought, 'Well, Lem don't seem so bad – not quite.' And Jud turned, his brutal, lowering face incredulous at what he was hearing.

'Yer what?' he thundered. 'What'n tarnation, Lem,' he began, then Lem hoisted the prisoner to his feet.

'Jud, he's deli-kate,' he said to Tex. 'I don't aim to let no deli-kate brother o' mine over-tire himself on you, hombre. Now I'm taking over.'

His last words came out swiftly, and a short chop-

ping blow jerked Tex's head way back on his spine.
Tex saw a slow grin come onto the scrub face of Jud
in appreciation of the crude humour of his brother.
Then up came that vicious, chopping right of Lem.

Lem didn't let him go. He held him with his left,
and chopped his face to ribbons with his right. When
Tex's weight proved too tiring, Lem let him drop.
But that was when Tex had been knocked stone cold
and wasn't feeling blows any more.

When he came to, the blood had dried on his face,
so that it was stiff and he felt he couldn't move.
Coming to consciousness was painful – so painful he
didn't want any of it, and several times he slipped
back into the dark before finally coming fully round.

Len and his brother had left him just where he had
dropped; they'd gone into the shade and were quietly
sleeping. 'Water,' Tex began to call, but they didn't
hear, perhaps because he couldn't hear the whisper so
plainly himself. He was pretty far gone by sunset,
when the two men rose, scratching and yawning.
While they made coffee again, they talked about him,
as if indifferent as to whether he heard them or not.

'Reckon we might jes' as well hyar the galoot,'
opined Jud.

Lem blew the thin twigs into flame and then
squatted, holding the coffee can handle across a
forked twig. 'Sure, why not? Ain't got nuthin' else ter
do. Reckon he'll feel like tellin' the truth after that
li'l ter-do we had.'

When the coffee was boiling he looked across at
Tex and said, 'You the sher'f's man? Or workin' fer
the railroad company?'

Tex shook his head slightly, speech being beyond
him.

'Can't talk, eh?' Lem grinned wolfishly, enjoying again his recent sadistic exertions. 'Reckon we'll have ter waste good water on the guy, Jed – he jes' can't speak no how, seems like.'

He was lavish with the water, though it was meant brutally. He fetched a canteen from the spring, then stood over the recumbent Texan and just emptied it over him. Tex had to drink what he could catch.

That was one drink the cowboy would remember all his life, however. The water was good and sweet, and bitingly cold to his inflamed face. It washed the blood away and revived him, and he felt that after all the sun hadn't sapped him completely of his strength – he thought, even then, that by God he'd find a way of getting outa this, and then ...

Not much went into his mouth, so he played possum, wanting more. When they tried to make him speak, he croaked so much they fetched him a canful to drink out of sheer exasperation. That canful finished off what the first had started – it made a new man of him, tied, battered and helpless though he was, here in the middle of the Texan desert.

Lem pulled the locket and chain out of his pants' pocket. There was a satisfied look in his eye as he played with it in his dirty, brutal paws. 'Good job fer us Milano Joe heered ye a-walkin' in our room,' he growled. 'He saw yer come out, pardner, an' when he tipped us off that a stranger who had ridden into town right on our heels was mighty interested in our belongin's, wal, it seemed we oughta do somethin' about it, yeah?'

40

'Didn't it occur to yer that I might be jes' some ornery sneak thief?'

'You didn't look the kind, stranger. Back in that thar saloon you looked mighty like a Ranger or a sher'ffs man to me.'

'Wal, I'm neither,' said Tex. He'd tell 'em the story from start to finish and see where that would lead him. After all, why not?

'I was on that train you stuck up,' he began calmly.

'How d'you know we stuck a train?' snapped Lem.

'That locket told me.'

'This yer? Know the gal, huh?'

'Seen her on the train, that's all. Reckernised her picture – her mother's, I s'pose.'

Lem nodded. 'An' how the tarnation blazes did yer get on our trail so soon?'

Tex tried to shrug, found it a painful business and didn't attempt it again. 'Jes' a hunch. Reckoned you wouldn't cross the Border, and struck out over the soft ground so's ter cut yer tracks. An' did it, too. Reckon I wasn't more'n a couple of hours behind you when you hit Milano Joe's dam' him.'

The next question came bleakly, with deathly intent and menace in the tone. 'Why?'

'Wal, I'll tell yer, though it'd be mighty generous of yer to set me free while I do it.'

'Stranger,' said Lem, 'I ain't gonna do it. You got muscles. Some muscles, stranger. No tellin' what y'd do with them if I set yer arms free.'

So Tex told his story. 'I was on that train. There was a li'l runt got het up when you found his wallet stuck in a shoe. When you'd gone he was that desprit to get it back, why lordy me, he ups and gives me

41

five hundred bucks an' sends me off after yer.'

'Musta been quite a bit o' dough in that wallet,' said Jud, sittin' up. Reflectively, 'Don't 'member no wallet with that air amount, do you, Lem?'

'No, guess I don't.'

'T'warn't money,' drawled the Texan. 'It was papers. Li'l guy's a senator, and he let on them papers was pretty powerful medicine. Looked ter me he meant bad medicine fer him, if they ever fell into wrong hands. So that's yer story, pards. That's why I beefed off after you. I ain't never stepped up five hundred bucks when it was pushed into my hand jes' for ridin' a horse and mebbe doin' a spot of gunnin' some time in consequence. An' the guy says thars another five hundred bucks a-comin' if I give him back his papers – unread.'

'Them papers sure sound mighty powerful medicine,' ruminated Lem, scratching his bristly chin. He spat into the fire. 'Wal, Jud, what yer thinkin'?'

'Who got the wallets? We shared out all the money, an' gave the wallets an' bags'n things ter Irish ter go and bury. D'you 'member seeing what he did with them?'

'Nope, reckon Irish is the only one that knows whar that wallet is.'

'Wal, Irish'll be ridin' in sometime termorrer. He'll tell us.'

'An' then what?' asked Tex.

'Then we'll do a spot of barter,' grinned Lem. 'Mebbe them papers is worth more than another five hundred bucks – in our hands.'

'Barter?' sneered Tex. 'Yer mean blackmail!' But he took care to say it to himself.

'What're we gonna do with him?' Jud asked.

Lem said, 'Aw, he c'n go fry. We'll keep him on hand till Irish comes termorrer, jes' ter see if Irish remembers anythin' 'bout papers.'

'Reckon that's something,' drawled Tex. 'Wal, how 'bout a li'l spot of grub, mister? I'm mighty peckish, I guess. Ain't eaten since late yesterday afternoon.'

Lem just said again, 'You go an' fry. You ain't gettin' no grub off'n us, stranger.'

'Shouldn't ha' come pokin' yer nose into other people's business,' was all that Jud had to say.

Some time later they rolled into their blankets and went to sleep. Tex waited until he knew they were well away and then began to roll towards the cache that he had spotted. In it, securely wrapped in cloth, was a hunk of bacon. The only other food not in cans was a sack of beans. Dried beans were no good to him as food, so he started on the cloth-covering of the bacon. By worrying like a dog he at length managed to shake the meat out of the folds. Then he lay full length, face into the bacon, and chewed it, raw.

Raw bacon isn't bad at any time, not unless you're from the city and squeamish. And the most tasty parts are the bits that are going off. When you're over a day behind with your diet, raw bacon's pretty tasty.

Tex ate pretty near three or four pounds of meat that night before calling it a day. That was a lot on an empty stomach, but Tex didn't see much food coming his way in the next day or so – if he managed to live that long. He'd long ago given up trying to get his hands free, and he didn't see much assistance coming this way out of the desert.

Then he rolled over to the spring and half fell in.

When the brothers woke next morning they found one cowboy who could go a full day without needing any further water.

'Wise guy,' said Lem, dragging him out.

'Fresh guy,' said Jud, and suddenly took a running kick that came near to stoving in the Texan's ribs. When Tex began to recover from that one he thought it was a good job that he'd been in hard training up North, otherwise this treatment would have been his lot. And then, pleasantly cool from his immersion, he spent two delightful hours dozing and thinking of the things he'd do to the brothers once he got out of this.

Somewhere before noon they heard the sound of horse's hooves ringing down the steep-walled canyon. Lem rose, grunting, 'Guess that'll be one of the boys.' He was pretty confident of this rocky hideout in the desert, but all the same his hands were on his guns as the rider cantered into sight.

'Pinky,' he said, shoving his guns back. Then he frowned. 'Pinky?' he said. 'Alone? Thought Irish'n Pinky went off together, Jud?'

'Sure did,' growled his brother. Then, as the rider came up, 'Howdy, Pinky. Whar's Irish?'

Pinky dismounted before replying. He was caked with the desert dust and seemed to have ridden far. When he turned Tex saw his face. There was something curious about the skin; it seemed to be tight, back of the ears, pulling the lips perpetually open so that his gums showed in a hard fixed grin. It reminded Tex of some of the hard fixed smiles he'd seen somewhat like that, only they been attached to dead hombres before.

Pinky said, 'What's this fellar?' and Lem growled.

'Jest a guy. He won't be stayin' long,' and that satisfied the newcomer.

'Irish?' asked Lem

'He got drunk and then took fight fever.' Pinky
swigged from the can before continuing. 'We kept to
the back trails, like you said, but when we came out
by Old Bull Crossing nothin' could keep that so-and-
so back but he'd go an' spend his dollars. That
Irishman sure got himself 'round a crate o' rye las'
night.'

'Did he talk?' – quickly, from Lem.

'A lot – but nary a word.' The brothers understood.
'He talked 'bout everything under the sun –
'specially fightin' – but kept off us.' Pinky paused
and looked significantly at Tex.

'Him?' said Jud, and kicked the helpless ex-
fighter to show he didn't count no more.

They squatted in the sand and drank thick coffee
while Pinky finished the tale. Irish had got in with
some pretty tough hombres who liked the fight
game. One of them said there was to be a big fight
down at Lozier that weekend, and at that nothing
would satisfy them but that they should all take the
train down.

'You tried to keep him back?'

'You ever tried to keep that mad Irishman back
when he's floating on alcohol?' Pinky's grin became
even more strained. 'Can't be done, Lem. An' when
thar's a fight as an added attraction, wal, guess you
might as well hold yer breath an' let him go. They
got the midnight express, the hull lot o' them, drunk
as coyotes that's found a barrel o' rum. Las' thing I
heard, they was shootin' holes through the train roof
ter let more air in.'

Tex came rolling over just then. A few things were beginning to click. 'Irish?' he said. 'Irish Mulloy?'

'You know him?' Lem didn't admit it, but it was good enough for Tex. He nodded.

'Sure do,' he said. 'Irish killed a fellar way back in Detroit, two-three months ago. Hit him with a stool, 'cause the fellar forgot he was supposed to flop in the fourth round. Mighty bad-tempered hombre, Irish.'

'That's him,' Pinky said, nodding. 'Now yer see why I didn't press like, when Irish decided on Lozier, last night. Know anything else 'bout Irish?'

'Only he came up the hard way – rail gangs, lumberjackin', bit o' herdin' in the Middle West. Got away with that killin' in Detroit 'cause the fellar didn't die till next day, an' by that time I guess Irish had caught a train some place.'

Like I did, he could have added. And he could have added, 'an' I was another o' the suckers they tried to drop before Irish.' Yeah, he'd been doing well, a coming fighter. Irish was a bit above him, but they weren't sure and gamblers like to make certain. So they said, 'Look, Tex, there's another century fer you if you'll just fold up nice and quiet like in the third or fourth round.'

That's when Tex had said, 'Nuthin' doin'. I don't fall down to any man.'

But they'd made sure, all the same. Just as Tex was leaving for the ring, a lump of angle iron that wasn't part of a fight arena's fittings and which didn't normally stand balanced right outside the door of any dressing room – well, it fell clean on to the muscles of his right shoulder. There was a guy helping it to fall, too, but it was all too late to start thinking of quitting.

46

He had gone into the ring hoping that the numbness would wear off. It hadn't. And Irish had played on to that shoulder from the first bell. By the end of round two it was murder. Irish, inflamed with the lust to kill, was hammering the one-handed cowboy with everything except the spit basin. Tex had gone down fighting, resisting while there was a spark of life left that could throw a glove. But he'd gone down. That had been just about as big a thrashing as he'd ever had in his life – just as big as the one those brothers had given him yesterday.

'He'll come back,' said Jud confidently. 'After the fight he'll remember where the jack comes from, an' you'll see him high-tailin' it across the desert.'

'If he don't get into no fight and get reckernised,' grinned Pinky significantly. 'Guess that's what the galoot will do. He'll be up in that ring a-challenging the champ. Irish ain't got no brains.'

'Cain't do nuthin' about it,' grumbled Lem. 'Jes' gotta wait here an' hope he comes through. Thar's some interestin' information we want from him, don't we, cowboy?'

Tex said nothing. He had an idea that if Irish didn't turn up for a week, then he'd have passed into the happy hunting grounds by that time.

Then they heard more hooves. This time the three bandits shot to their feet. There was panic in the sound, an urgency in the flying feet that carried an alarm to them.

Tucson Tommy came belting round the bend as if all the Injuns in hell were on his trail. He pulled his horse to a flying halt, feet rearing to the sky, body covered with lather. Before he had halted, Tucson was shouting at them.

"Get yer horses! Ride, ride!'

'What'n the hell?' roared Lem, but all the same they were tightening girths and slinging on their kit.

'It's the Mexicans. They're over the Border agen,' shouted Tucson, wheeling. 'Must be the Pancho gang. Thar's a coupla hundred of 'em, at least. I saw 'em behind me all this last hour.'

'Did they see you?' Lem was swinging on to his plunging horse.

'Don't reckon so, they was trottin' easy. But thar ain't no mistake. It's hyar they're headin' fer. My horse ain't fresh like yourn. I'm off.'

Tucson lashed his mount and went tearing North into the cactus-covered desert. Half a minute later Pinky and Jud swung up beside their leader.

'What about that guy?' Pinky called.

'Him? He don't count,' said Lem callously, 'Them Mexes'll know how to look after him.' Then they plunged spurs into quivering, terrified horseflesh and plunged after Tucson.

Tex sat up, sweating. He hadn't lain immersed in water all night for nothing. It had been torture, while the ropes swelled, but it meant that today when they dried they'd come a bit looser.

Tex guessed that, given half an hour or so, he'd manage to get one hand out, though maybe it would-n't have much skin on by the time he'd got the rough rope over ...

But Tex knew that he didn't have half an hour. From the sound of it, the Mexicans couldn't be more than ten or fifteen minutes' ride away, and he wasn't going to be there when they came in for water.

When you have wars between peoples it leaves

scars and sores. This recent war between the State of Texas and Mexico hadn't been bloody, according to some standards, but it had been bitter, and both sides were still hating each other's guts even though the politicians had managed to get a peace treaty signed.

Tex knew that if Mexican marauders found him alone and helpless, it wouldn't be pleasant for him. Those bloodthirsty peons knew things that civilised people were trying to forget ...

Tex started up the side of the rock, lying on his back and pressing himself upwards from his heels. He must have looked like a landed seal, but that moment he didn't care how he looked. After a while, maybe ten or twelve feet above the floor of the canyon, he saw a cleft in the rock face. He rolled over and dropped in, hoping there weren't no rattlers.

Two or three minutes later he heard the jingling of harness, as the Mexican marauders came cantering up to the spring. Tex thought grimly, 'any moment now,' and waited for some keen-eyed Mexican to come and investigate the scratching on the wall face.

CHAPTER FOUR

EXIT ONE RIDER

Tex didn't waste his energy in a furious attempt to get rid of his bonds now that the new enemy had appeared. Anyway, he had hardly any energy left in his long-bound arms as it was.

Steadily, persistently, he worked on them. If he failed, he knew that that was his end, and someday someone would be puzzled by the discovery of a skeleton nicely tucked away in a crack in the rock face. Only that would be long after a buzzard had found him and picked his bones clean. That buzzard up there now, for instance.

He heard rapid talk, as if the newcomers were interested in the fresh track marks; then some went galloping off, and Tex guessed that they had gone to try and find out who had so recently been using this sandy-floored canyon.

Some time later one hand came free; an hour later he was entirely rid of the ropes that had kept him so close company for nearly forty-eight hours. For the next three hours he just lay there, allowing the circulation to come back into his hands and feet. His feet soon recovered, but his hands – that was torture. As the blood came pulsing through arteries and veins that had been squashed near closed, it was like the distilled venom of a thousand wasps coming over open nerve-ends. How he stood it without crying out aloud he never knew.

But he did.

To get out of this desert he knew he must have a horse. If they went and left him here, he'd have to stay until the food ran out, because he knew he could never safely cover the surrounding waste on foot. Without a horse, death seemed sure, one way or another.

Tex guessed it was no use trying to steal a horse under cover of darkness – these Mexicans were like cats, and they'd hear him. Horses won't go on tip-toe, even when your life depends on it.

The Mexicans were obviously camping for the night, for look-outs were posted at both ends of the canyon.

Tex watched the sentries change during the night – watched especially the one that rode away back round the bend to guard the far end of the canyon. He was a *hombre* who was going to die.

The big cowboy spent most of the night inching his way along the rock wall to an overhang forty or fifty yards or so away. He made it without attracting any attention from the sleeping camp, and then dozed off to sleep himself.

When he awoke the camp was stirring and preparing food for breakfast. Very soon after that they began mounting, preparatory to a move off.

The leader, extravagantly dressed in richly

51

embroidered clothing, sombreroed and red-sashed, whistled between his fingers. The guard down the canyon shouted something in reply, and Tex heard the horse's hooves trotting towards him.

He looked at the Mexicans. They were milling around, trying to get out of each other's way, trying to get out into the open desert. There was much shouting, mostly genial but some bad-tempered. Nobody seemed to be looking back.

The Mexican sentry came cantering up to the overhang. Tex dived into him, crashing him to the sandy ground. He never spoke a word, that Mexican, because all the way from the saddle until he hit the ground there was a hand gripping his throat; and when they touched floor another hand came up and a Mexican was squeezed slowly off the earth.

And no one seemed to have noticed.

Tex glanced up. The band was riding slowly away. Probably a fold in the ground hid most of their bodies, anyway. The horse had gone careering for a few yards and then had stopped for a drink at the spring.

Tex took the dead hombre's guns, stuck his hat on his head, and openly walked across to the horse. If anyone bothered to look back now they'd sure think he was the Mex, he thought.

The cowboy pulled the cayuse back out of sight and let the band ride away into the distance. He waited, expecting a shout of alarm any moment, but minutes passed and none came.

He'd made it!

He got water and raided the cache, then mounted. He went from that canyon faster than he should have done, considering the long way ahead, but he didn't like that place. It reminded him of death too much. All the time he'd been there, he'd been thinking of death. His own. Now he was thinking of Lem and Jud.

Still death ...

He followed the single track that looked like Pinky's, for he knew it had come from a rail town, and he wanted to get to the railway as fast as he could. He hit Old Bull Crossing just after sundown, and learned that he had to wait another day for the train to Lozier, but he'd still be in the Border capital in time for the big fight.

A rest for a whole day did him good anyway. Physically he was in superb condition, and though he had taken the hammering of his life in the last few days, only his face showed it when he climbed aboard the midnight express – his limbs had suppled up, and the bruises were forgotten.

The train, crawling through that seemingly endless countryside of thorn scrub and knee-high mesquite grass, was due in Lozier by ten the next morning. At exactly nine o'clock Tex saw the girl again.

She came into the diner where Tex was trying to persuade a breakfast out of a negro attendant who didn't intend to be persuaded short of a dollar tip. He recognised her but saw that she didn't recognise his battered countenance. So when she sat down he ambled over to her and said, 'See, honey, my eyes is in mourning, 'cause they reckoned they'd seen the last o' you.'

It took the startled girl a good ten seconds to remember where she'd seen that face before, then she said, unoriginally, 'You!'

'Me,' said Tex. 'How come you all travelling back

the way you went so quickly?'

'I had every blamed dollar taken off me that night you all stood tryin' to touch the ceiling,' snapped the girl. 'Remember?'

'Reckon I do,' said Tex imperturbably. 'Reckon I 'member other things 'bout that night, too. Someone callin' me a coward, 'cause I didn't go'n commit suicide on a bullet.'

The girl gave a cold little shrug and turned to look out of the window. 'Down in Lozier men seem to take bigger risks,' she merely answered. 'As it is, I went all that way, stayed two nights on borrowed money, then had to come back. It should have been a month's holiday.'

'Tough,' said Tex. 'Still, I reckon I know where that locket of yourn is.'

That brought her to her feet. She was round in a flash. Plainly that locket was a treasured possession and she had grieved to lose it. He saw her excited face, her blue, enquiring eyes. Saw what a pretty gal she was, and it seemed that he saw her for the first time in that moment.

'You know—' she began, and then her eyes narrowed with suspicion. 'Stranger,' she snapped, 'I've a hunch you're stringing me.'

'I ain't no stranger, ma'am,' said the cowboy calmly. 'You met Tex McQuade afore, didn't you — Lavender Grey?'

She stared at him, her eyes big and round and perplexed. 'Why, you know my name!'

'Yes, ma'am, it was on that picture in that locket o' yourn. Honest, I ain't kiddin'. I seen it. In fact, fer one blessed hour I had the blamed thing in my shirt pocket.'

'But what happened? Why did you let it go again?'

Tex grinned wryly and pointed to his battered face. 'See that? Wal, I reckon I got that 'cause I lit on yer locket. That air locket o' yourn sure brought me heap plenty trouble.'

The girl said, 'If you want me to grab those puffed-up ears of yours, cowboy, and shake your head – keep right on talking in riddles.'

Tex crowed, 'A gal with spirit. Oh, shake me, Lavender Grey, shake me, honey child!'

'Oh, Tex, have a heart,' she pleaded, changing her tactics and becoming at once frail woman appealing to big-hearted man. 'Tell me about my locket. If only you can help me get it back.'

So Tex told her. Not all the story – about Senator Hooker, for instance – that wasn't necessary. But about Lem and Jud and Pinky and the other gangsters he had so nearly got a rope on – and who had so nearly got a noose on him, too. He mentioned Irish, but not much about him; and he didn't tell her why he was travelling to Lozier. She was only interested in Lem and Jud and the locket they'd filched.

'I wonder, Tex, will I ever get it back again, do you think?' she asked wretchedly, 'I – I suppose Lem's keeping it so's to give it to some girl friend of his.'

'S'pose so,' agreed Tex. 'Still, reckon I might meet up with it at that. I ain't given up this trail yet, and I think if I follow Irish, in the end I'll be crossing Friends Lem and Jud agen.' He lifted his head and his eyes were hard as they stared unseeingly beyond her. 'I'll meet up with 'em,' he whispered, 'if it's the last thing I do!'

He felt the girl shudder, and pulled himself together. 'Tex,' she said, 'you should have seen your eyes. They must have done terrible things to you.'

'They did,' he agreed, and then became his old, bantering humorous self again.

Lozier came. Perhaps it came too soon for them. And a buggy was waiting for her, and with it her father – tall and lean, with drooping moustaches like the inverted horns of the cattle he reared back along the Border grass belt. A Southerner of the old school, by the slowness of his speech.

They were introduced, they spoke; but the old man was suspicious and whisked his daughter away from the tough-looking hombre she'd met on the train. But as Tex helped her into the high seat, Lavender Grey turned for a second, smiled a smile that would have brought a man a hundred miles, and whispered, 'It's the Two-by-Two, Tex. And only ten miles or so!'

'My gawsh,' said Tex, hatless, staring at the dust as the buggy spanked swiftly down the dusty street. 'Ef that warn't an in-vite-ation, then I ain't no McQuade. An' maybe I'll accept it at that.'

But before then, he had business to do. He had to find Irish.

Even before that, he had to find a room; and that was difficult because the town was full of fight fans. Bang outside the station was a big poster which told the world – or at any rate, the fight world – that Killer Lenski, acknowledged world heavyweight champion, would meet Bull Sertza, pride and champ of Texas. It was apparent that the meeting was much to the satisfaction not only of Lozier but also most of the other Border towns; for this appeared to be the biggest fight that had ever been staged on the Frontier.

Tex got a room. As a room it wasn't anything, but it gave him a place to sleep in. Then he began a search of the town.

Lozier's no small place. It is the biggest town on the Texas-Mexican border, and has a population running into six figures. After one hour of finding that Lozier had more than one main street, and that there were hundreds of small streets in the background, Tex just about gave it up. It seemed hopeless, like picking a needle out of a bale of hay.

He tried the saloons, but he didn't recognise Irish, and there was a limit to the amount he could drink, so he just drifted. It was the same next day, the day of the big fight. Drifting from place to place, hoping always to see the shaggy flaming mop of the bruiser from Detroit – and never meeting up with him.

There were too many people, far too many, but all the same, Tex had to find the Irishman, if it were at all possible. If he failed to get on his trail here, in Lozier, it seemed as though he could say good-bye to his chances of picking up those other five hundred dollars – and get his revenge on the brothers who had treated him so brutally!

Around noon papers came on to the street and provided excitement. Men swore as they read – Mexican marauders had slipped across the Border in force and had left a fiery trail as deep as fifty miles inland. Ranch after ranch had been attacked and gone up in flames. Men and women had died with their children; stock had been stampeded, fences torn down, feed set on fire – in general a train of havoc had cut a crescent swathe little more than a hundred miles west of Lozier.

Tex knew who was responsible – Pancho and his

Mexicans. He must have seen them at the start of their raid.

All around him angry Texans were whipping themselves into an ugly mood, ripe for any mischief. Mexicans in the town suddenly found it healthier to stay indoors or get to hell out of the place. After a time Tex saw a great crowd beginning to form up in a procession which started off for the Governor's House.

'What's the idea, pard?' asked Tex of one of the marchers.

'We're gonna demand an end to the armistice,' he shouted. 'We ain't gonna stand by an' see a little Mexican army comin' burnin' an' killin' all the time thar's supposed to be peace a-tween our countries. Come an' join us, cowboy; reckon we'll need them shooters o' yourn.'

But Tex had other business to do. Until then he had put in every waking minute on the street, hoping to bump into Irish, but now he decided he had better report to the senator at the Hotel Mexicana. He hadn't wanted to do it; he'd been anxious to put it off as long as possible. For, to date, he hadn't much success to report.

The senator was in, and Tex was taken up without delay. The paunchy Hooker met him at the door. 'Shuck's, ol' Hooker's mighty anxious 'bout them papers,' was Tex's first thought.

'D'you get them?'

Tex shook his head. The senator's eyes looked evil.

'Then what the are you doin' here? I gave you money to get on the trail of those men. If you've come expecting more money without results, you're mighty hopeful.'

Tex shoved back his hat, his jaw setting. He wasn't going to take that sort of talk from any city hombre just because he thought his money all-powerful.

'Senator,' he said gently, 'ef I have any more o' that sort of talk from you I guess I'll get powerful angry. I didn't come fer no money. I'm on the trail o' them crooks, an' it's led me hyar ter Lozier. One of 'em's hyar, an' he's the only one that knows whar them papers is hidden.'

That made a difference. The senator shot out question after question, eager for any information which might suggest that the papers would be recovered. But Tex could hardly add to his hopes. He made his report, then went. Minutes were precious, and he guessed that he had less than fifteen or eighteen hours before Irish lit out once again from the town.

But the quest seemed hopeless. At nine that night, when almost every man in Lozier was converging on the arena, he still hadn't seen him. Tex went with the crowd, too; Irish wouldn't be in the town now – he'd be here somewhere in the arena.

But when Tex went into that great bowl and saw fifty or sixty thousand people under the flaming lights, he recognised that he hadn't a Chinaman's chance of spotting Mulloy, big though he was.

After a while he got up and went round to the dressing rooms. Tex had decided on a long shot, one way of making the Irishman come and look for him – Tex McQuade.

The first two preliminary fights ended quickly. Perhaps that's why the promoter decided to do as

Tex suggested. In the interval after the second bout, the promoter, perspiring in his white shirt under the strong arc-lights, called for attention from the restive crowd. He started to read from a scrap of paper.

'I have a message for a hombre called Irish Mulloy.' He waited, as if expecting Irish to stand up and take a bow. But nothing happened. 'It's from a hombre named Tex McQuade. McQuade's here ternight, an' he sez he'll beat Mulloy from high hell ter breakfast time, in a fair fight.'

Again a pause, and the crowd held its breath. But Mulloy sat fast, if he was there among them. Maybe he thought this was a trap. So the fight promoter went on, 'McQuade sez as how Mulloy beat him in a framed fight last time in Detroit. He sez he don't need ter drop no lumps of iron on his opponent's shoulders ter make the fight even.'

And Irish Mulloy sat fast even at that insult. Tex, waiting and watching, despaired. Maybe Irish wouldn't respond at all. Maybe he wasn't there, even – maybe lying drunk, the fight he'd come to see forgotten, in some squalid bar. The promoter made his last throw.

'McQuade tells me ter say that Mulloy's a dirty, low-down, stinkin' polecat, jes a nacheral, no good maverick with no title to a fightin' name. McQuade sez—'

But he didn't need to go any further. By now he'd stung Mulloy into an anger that blinded him to any question of safety.

'Tell McQuade I'll knock the livin' lights outa him!" roared a voice, and then the crowd went mad as the huge, lumbering red-head rose from his seat and started to crash his way towards the ring. Here was a fight they would enjoy – a malice match. They were up on their toes in an instant, rooting for the contestants.

Tex was there before him, peeling off his shirt. This would be a fight without bother of fighting trunks – just pants on and shirts off. A second came up with gloves, and Tex went towards him.

Irish came swinging through the ropes, hurling his shirt among the ringside spectators. 'Look after that,' he called. 'I'll be back fer it in a minute!' The crowd cheered like mad again. That was fighting talk.

Tex turned as he heard the other's boots stamping into the ring. He had a vision of a great gorilla chest, red-haired, flaming mad face thrusting towards him.

He wasn't ready for it. The crowd screamed a warning. Then Tex went flying through the ropes, his face smashed open by a tremendous hook from his bare-fisted opponent.

CHAPTER FIVE

PINKY STOPS SOME LEAD

Tex somehow staggered up. Around him was pandemonium. The crowd was on its feet, screaming and catcalling at the treacherous blow. Up in the ring the big bruiser from Detroit stood and defied the lot of them, his face aflame no less than his hair – stood and snarled and cursed and invited anyone to come and take Tex's place in the ring.

But Tex didn't need any substitute. A mighty roar came up from the crowd as they saw his figure clamber back into the ring. The referee and seconds tried to get control of the bout and stood between the contestants. But Irish wouldn't wear gloves, so Tex wasn't having any, either.

The referee started talking about three-minute rounds and fighting fair, but everyone knew that what he said didn't mean a thing. The seconds got out; Irish charged like a mad bull. The crowd stood and roared, and plainly they wanted to see the tall cowboy get his own back for that act of treachery.

Tex side-stepped the rush. That first blow had dazed him, and he wanted time to recover. Irish came wheeling and charged again. This time he was too quick for the Texan, too quick and strong. Tex found those mighty, red-haired arms come crashing through his guard, seeking out the cuts and bruises on his face, and deliberately opening them again.

Within a minute of the fight starting, blood was streaming into his eyes, into his mouth. He could hardly see. Somewhere a trace of humour lurked even now, and he thought, 'I've bin bustin' to meet Irish all yesterday and terday. Now – heck, mebbe I should ha' kept out o' the galoot's way!'

The trouble was, he couldn't. While the crowd howled encouragement that did him no good, Tex went back and back round the ring, desperately trying to shield his bleeding face from those ponderous, murderous blows. Up to now he'd hardly had chance to get a punch in. Maybe he should have stalled, after that first wicked punch, and waited until his head completely cleared.

'A stinkin' polecat, am I?' growled Irish. 'A disgrace to the Old Sod, you say – you durned horse-totin' Irishman, you! Take that!'

Tex took it. He couldn't help it. It was a blow that came over and caught him flush on the right cheekbone and smashed him to the canvas.

The crowd sank back. This was the end. As a malice match it hadn't been anything to shout about, after all.

Maybe that hit the red-head. Maybe the silence, when he'd been expecting the cheers that usually go to the victor, inflamed him to an unnecessary act of vindictiveness. Shoving the counting referee on one side, he drove his riding boot into the fallen cowboy's ribs.

The crowd screamed. The referee jumped forward to intervene. Irish whirled and knocked the referee round the ring and into a corner. Then he came jumping back at the groaning Tex.

Tex saw him coming, and now there was murder in the puncher's heart. That was the dirtiest trick! This time, he swore, he'd make Irish pay for it. And curiously the extent of his indignation seemed to clear that spinning head of his, in some way his eyes came back to focus where before they'd seen only a blur.

Irish didn't see the change in his opponent; he was completely reckless now and let drive again to Tex's ribs.

Tex saw the foot crashing towards him ... rolled and caught it and heaved all in one motion. Irish seemed to rise into the air, a look of surprise on his face, and then toppled over the ropes.

The crowd just about went hysterical. A crowd loves to see a man come from the brink of defeat and snatch victory when it is least expected. And their sympathies clearly were with the big puncher, and unmistakably hostile towards Irish.

It took a couple of minutes to get Mulloy out of the wreckage of the ringside seats on which he had fallen, and when he came back into the ring there was an ugly cut along his forehead. It evened things up, and also gave Tex a chance to recover.

Tex saw that Mulloy's legs were still wobbly, and streaked in. Irish snarled and lashed out like a cat. Tex took the blow on his ribs, and in turn connected with a quick one-two to the face.

And now the Texan had confidence enough to put his original plan into action. As he danced away, he jeered, 'I ain't the only one that thinks yore a stinkin' polecat. Lem an' Jud Cole's got that idea, too.'

Irish dropped his guard in astonishment at hearing those names in the middle of the fight ring. Tex crashed in with a barrage of blows that had the red-head reeling into the ropes before he could find strength to make a come-back.

Tex danced out of range again – and talked once more. 'Sure, an' Tucson an' Pinky don't think much to yer neither. Pinky sez yore a squarehead an' a palooka. That's why they're cuttin' you out of that deal.'

'What deal?' Irish spat through bloody lips to show his contempt, but he was listening hard.

'Yore proper share o' the train loot.' That got through the red-head's guard, too. The train loot – this guy seemed to know everything. Before he had time to recover, the wily Texan smashed him to his knees with a right to the mouth. Now Irish found himself tiring, not getting up so quickly. The crowd roared its appreciation. Why, durn it, this was probably better stuff than they'd see in the big fight!

When he rose, swaying, Tex was circling, talking behind those punishing fists. 'Yeah, you sucker. 'Member when you went and stuck them useless wallets away? Well, they was watching. And them wallets wasn't so useless at that. Some o' them papers was valuable, but they didn't let on to you. They wanted them papers fer themselves. Now they're planning ter go an' collect 'em durin' this week, when they figger it'll be safe ter get back inter that part o' the country agen.'

Irish looked at him, but Tex saw that he had fallen for the crude story. In his eyes was a slow suspicion; Irish was ready to believe that there had been a double-cross by his pardners. 'By God,' he gritted, 'when I get my hands on them double-dyed no good ...'

But Tex came in to the attack just then. This fight had slowed up while he got the idea he wanted into Irish's head. Now he could forget about finesse and indulge in a little hate. The red-head was strong and formidable, and he had a hard fight on his hands.

They still talk about that fight in Lozier and along the Border. Two bare-fisted men stood and swapped punches, toe to toe. Rounds were ignored, rules went by the board. It was a contest of smash and be smashed, and the weakest in the end would go down.

But it was a long time before the delirious crowd saw who was weakening. And when it was seen to be Irish that was tottering before the fury of the berserk young Texan, they nearly took the roof off – only there was no roof. The end came suddenly. Tex, too, was weakening, and he knew he had to find strength for that final knock-out. He closed his eyes for a second while his opponent climbed to his feet following a fall, and he thought of all the things that this gol-darned gang had done to him. It was only for second but it was enough.

Irish looked up and saw his opponent with his eyes closed, as if out on his feet. Triumph chased away bewilderment, and with a roar he charged. It was his last charge.

Tex hit him in the middle of his run, and the red-head went down as if pole-axed.

Back in the dressing room the world champ heard the cheers and growled, 'What gives? Which is de champ, me or de guy that won dat bout?'

They had to carry Irish to the dressing room, but Tex managed to walk – just. In his heart was a tremendous satisfaction. He had thrashed one of the gang, and if his hunch wasn't wrong he'd soon be trailing Irish back to where those papers were hidden.

There was a train going out around mid-after-noon next day. It was the Tombstone Flyer. Waking that morning Tex had had ideas on riding out on a hired horse to the Two-by-Two ranch. ('It's only ten miles'), but one look at his puffed and blackened eyes was enough for him.

'Ain't gonna let no gal see me ownin' a face like this,' he decided, then stiffly prepared for his jour-ney back to the Border town where he'd left his horse – and where he guessed Irish's horse would be, too.

He was careful to keep out of sight when he saw Irish crawl painfully into Lozier station. Irish was dumb, but not so dumb that he wouldn't start asking questions if he saw Tex on the same train.

Tex ignored the Pullman; instead he clambered into a horse-wagon that didn't have any horses, heaved an armful of hay into the manger, and went blissfully to sleep in it.

He was feeling a whole lot better when it was time to alight. It was ten and dark, and he leaned out of the truck and watched the broad-shouldered Irish Mulloy cross the pool of light that was the station, then he jumped down and followed.

The next few minutes were the most anxious ones for Tex. If Irish lit out in the dark it would be impossible for the cowboy to follow his trail until daylight. Now, if only the thick-headed hombre would decide to sleep off some more of his stiffness ...

He did. Tex watched him enter the solitary hotel; he waited quarter of an hour, and no horseman came from the stables. Then Tex decided it was safe to find sleep, and the liveryman let him use a bale of hay above where his horse was stabled.

When morning came, the Texan felt so good he could have swapped more punches with the red-head. His stiffness was wearing off, though his eyes seemed not a bit less blacker.

The cowboy had his Mexican horse all saddled and ready for the trail when Irish came riding slowly down from the hotel. Standing in the shadow of the livery stable, Tex could see without being seen. And he grinned as he saw a battered face that matched his own. If anything, Irish was in worse condition than he was, and judging by the way he jerked on the reins, his temper was certainly much different.

Tex let him get well ahead, then discreetly followed. Irish wasn't easy trail, because, back in the saddle again, he seemed to become more alert, more suspicious than he had been in the shelter of the towns.

The only way to follow him was to take risks. Tex let his late opponent disappear completely from sight over the horizon, and then race hard after him. From the brow of that distant hill he reined and stayed hidden until Irish disappeared again over the next brow. It was hard on the Mexican pony, but it was tough and seemed to stand up well to the strain of the swift galloping.

About a couple of hours on the trail, Tex lost him. He guessed that Irish must have taken to the open desert, obeyed a hunch that he had turned north and not southwards, and cut across in a wide arc. It was an hour later before he found the trail again

Now it was a question of tracking. Most times it was easy, in the soft sand, but occasionally there were troublesome patches, where Irish had crossed bare rock. Then Tex had to lean from the saddle, his eyes questing like an Injun's for a scratch on the surface, a chip out of the rock – the merest indication that he was heading right.

Soon the distant outline of hills, low and purple, began to take shape through the haze that shimmered up from the white and arid desert. After a while Tex spotted a familiar landmark, and knew that they were heading back towards the rail track. He felt that they must be near to the cache by now; about here the gang must have split their loot and then parted company, he thought.

Suddenly he pulled quickly on the reins. The tracks of several horsemen had appeared from down a dry creek bed, and had joined the solitary rider's. Tex saw that these horsemen were following Irish Mulloy because their broncs were obliterating the solitary trail.

His eyes narrowed as he looked down, examining every mark for the story they could tell.

'Four tracks,' he ruminated. 'Could be Lem, Jud, Pinky an' Tucson.' But he wanted confirmation. Sometimes other punchers came into the desert to round up strays and mavericks, or these tracks might be Mexes', too. Then Tex saw that one of the horses had a slurred track from its right foreleg – it came from a characteristic sideways kick as it trotted. The track looked familiar to the cowboy, like one he'd followed that day to Milano Joe's ...

That settled it. These four horsemen were the remaining members of the train-robbing gang.

But something puzzled the cowboy. How come they were trailing Irish? It didn't add up straight. They didn't know that Irish had had suspicion thrown into his mind, sending him searching for some valuable papers that he had carelessly thrown away or hidden in the desert. Yet they were trailing him as if they knew; as if they knew and wanted to see where he led them.

Tex sat and worked that one out, because he couldn't make hide nor horns of it. All he could think of was that after the Mexicans had pushed them out of their distant hide-out, they must have holed up somewhere farther south. That had put them within sight of Irish when he came riding back. They'd seen him in the distance, and probably the suspicious Lem had said, 'What's that hombre up to? He should be ridin' north instead of west.' And that suspicion would be sufficient to get the four desperadoes mounting and quietly following.

Tex didn't know it, but his guess wasn't far off the mark.

He came on cautiously now, breasting each rise at a slow walk, guns ready and so he came out upon the final drama, so far as Irish was concerned.

Suddenly he reined atop a short bluff. Below he was in time to see the gang riding out on to the surprised Irish. He had dismounted and appeared to have pulled something white that was bulky from within a thorn bush. From where he was Tex decided that the white thing could be a pillowcase.

Voices drifted up quite clearly to the cowboy's ears. First Lem's rough challenge. 'What're you up to, Irish?'

Then Irish, 'What're you up to, you mean?' Irish had dropped the bag and had gone into a crouch. 'So you were goin' ter double-cross me, huh?'

'Looks mighty like someone else was planning a double-cross,' snarled Lem. From above Tex could se that they were all crouching now in their saddles, and he knew that at any moment hell was going to be let loose.

'I know yer game,' suddenly shouted Irish, mad with fury at the thought that he had been allowed to walk into a trap set by his former pards. 'But you won't get me …'

It was a bad prophecy.

They all got him. Probably the beating he had taken the previous night had slowed up his gun arm.

Irish's Colt came out flaming, but there were slugs tearing his life apart even before the barrel had been raised towards his adversaries. Jud's two guns thundering out a death roar … Lem's cracking murder … Pinky's and Tucson's screaming leaden death. Four men pumping hot lead into one too slow to draw.

Tex saw the huge red-headed boxer swing round as the slugs smacked into his bulk, saw his bruised and battered face drop open as if in surprise at something unbelieved until now. Saw it register acknowledgement that death had called to claim him.

And that was the end of the trail for Irish Mulloy.

Jud callously shoved the bleeding hulk on one side and dropped down to examine the contents of the pillowcase.

Lem followed, and then the other two joined in curiously.

Tex heard odd words of discussion, but couldn't catch what they meant. One thing after another was looked at and discarded, then finally they seemed to concentrate upon one thing. Tex saw a paper being handed round, and guessed they'd found the senator's wallet. More, they seemed to have learned the secret that the wallet had contained, the secret that the senator seemed anxious not to become public property.

'They know more'n I know,' thought Tex, upon the brow, and his curiosity was piqued and he would have given his ears to know what was on those papers that the gang seemed so interested in.

But that thought was lost in a more urgent one. The gang were now in possession. How could he hope to get them away from four desperate men?

He knew that if they started off on their trail again, his quest would be pretty hopeless. You can't hope to follow a desperate gang of bandits for more than a few hours without being detected. And four against one ... He looked at Irish, and could imagine what his own fate would be if this gang caught him tailing them.

After a moment he turned and rode a few yards down a sandy gulch, and then dismounted. He was going to try and get those papers, though the odds were four to one against him.

It wasn't altogether the money that he'd get for the papers if he were successful. He had a score to settle against these outlaws, and he might never again get an opportunity to meet up with them.

So he came boldly, openly into the hollow where they stood, his cowboy boots sinking deep and silently into the shifting sand. They didn't hear him, so engrossed were they in the papers, so sure that no one was near in this vast, sun-blistered, cactus-spotted land of rolling sand hills.

When he was no more than twenty paces away, he spoke. 'Don't move!'

They froze instantly into immobility. It was almost comical how they held their positions as the words caught them — Jud half-bent so that his shadow didn't fall on the fluttering paper in his two hands, Lem in the act of hitching up his pants, Pinky and Tucson with their heads together in argument.

Then, his words dropping like cracking icicles, Tex rapped, 'Up with yer hands! Turn slowly and don't get standing behind each other!'

Slowly their hands went up, slowly they turned. Tex heard a gasp of recognition. 'By thunder, you!'

'Me,' said Tex grimly. 'But it's no thanks to you that I'm alive!'

There was exultation in his heart. It was true that he hadn't got away with it yet, but up to now it had turned out to be surprisingly easy. Ridiculously easy. He'd got the four desperadoes at his mercy!

'Lem,' he said, his voice grating, 'you get them papers from Jud an' put 'em all together in that wallet you're holdin'. Then give it ter me.'

'An' then?' Lem had said. He glared back at the cowboy, and almost it seemed as though he was ready to throw himself on to the gun and risk extinction.

'Then,' said Tex, 'we'll see about things.' For the truth was, he didn't know what the heck to do with them. It would be too dangerous, single-handed, to march the quartet off the desert to some Border jail; they'd sure turn the tables on him somehow. The safest thing ... the only thing ... to do was to kill them where they stood, with their hands up.

But he knew he couldn't do that.

The situation was solved for him. Lem turned abruptly to his brother and held out his hand for the papers. Jud grunted nastily, but handed them over. Lem stuffed them into the wallet and stepped forward.

Too late Pinky realised that the bandit-leader was prepared to sacrifice his, Pinky's, life for his own. Lem suddenly pulled the unprepared Pinky into the line of fire and dived for his gun.

Tex, startled by the move, had a vision of Jud hurtling sideways, of Tucson falling to his knees and drawing. Tex blasted at Lem, trying to hit his exposed gun hand, but the slug entered Pinky and the train-robber screamed as it tore into his stomach. He got the next two or three slugs, because Tex had to stop that gun of Lem's from bursting up on him, and then Pinky quit screaming just as suddenly as he had started. Lem's gun went blazing off, but it wasn't within miles of the back-tracking cowboy, because the dead weight of Pinky sent him falling backwards.

Jud got sand in his face from a stream of bullets,

and a lucky shot smashed the shoulder of Tucson and put him out of action with his right arm.

All that happened in the space of, probably, five seconds. And in that time Tex knew that he had failed. He knew that Lem and Jud would in seconds have the drop on him, and then they'd saw him in half with their guns.

Swift as lightning, he holstered one gun and went crabbing away round a hillock of sand on two legs and an arm. He was an elusive, quick-shifting target, and in addition his left gun was throwing lead and disconcerting his opponents aim. The last thing he saw as he rolled out of sight was Tucson Tommy, gun in his left hand, blood bathing his chest, staggering towards him with the firmest intention of despatching him right out of this earth.

For the brief moment out of sight, Tex bent double and hared as fast as his long legs could take him up that shifting sandy gulch, to where his horse was standing. A surprised horse felt him take a leap straight into the saddle, and then, whinnying with fear, it bolted up the gulch.

Tex heard a gun roaring behind and bullets whizzed past his head. Then distinctly he heard one smack into his mount, heard the impact and felt the horse falter in its stride. Tex looked down. What he saw made him sure that this was one horse that would never run another race.

Tex kept on its back for another hundred yards or so, down the other side of the hill. His horse was faltering badly now. He guessed that Lem and Jud, if not Tucson also, would have gone for their mounts and be rapidly catching up.

A thick scrub-thorn showed up, and Tex dived

headlong behind it from his flying horse. Once behind he didn't move. That bush was too thin to give adequate cover.

Lem came bursting over the sandy brow, followed closely by Jud and then, a good half-minute later, by the wounded Tucson, swaying in the saddle but determined not to be out of the kill.

Tex let them go by, then jumped out on to the trampled sand and raced back towards the top of the short hill. Slipping over it where a bush hid his figure from making a skyline silhouette, Tex dropped on his face and, panting, looked back. What he saw made him realise that in fact Tucson's bullet had saved his life.

CHAPTER SIX

POWERFUL PAPER
MEDICINE

His horse had foundered. Tex could see it over on its side down among the prickly pears and cactus. He saw Lem and the others weaving in and out of the scrub towards it. Saw them halt when they reached the still horse, halt and look around, and then gallop on just another hundred yards further in a circling movement that was designed to entrap him afoot.

Saw them break through the scrub and come out into the open of a broad, sandy, dry-creek bed. Saw them ride right into the middle of a crescent moon of silent, mounted Mexican raiders, just waiting for them to walk into their arms.

From above Tex watched it all. The horns of the crescent moved and closed in around the three riders. Lem and Jud were about to fire, when a word of command crackled out and stayed their hands. It was enough. Half-a-dozen nearly naked Mexicans were on to each rider in a flash, dragging them to earth.

Tex had an impulse to turn and run, but there was just a chance that the Mexicans hadn't counted the number who had come over the hill and so didn't know he was there. He dug in at that. Anyway, he might just as well sell his life here, where he had a good position at the head of the slope, as take to the flatter country beyond where they'd easily run him down.

They weren't gentle with the prisoners. Tex saw them being dragged to where their leader sat astride his horse. The distance was great, but it seemed to Tex that he was the same Mexican that he'd seen the previous week at the bandits' hideout. If so, this was probably the celebrated Pancho the Mexican, the Border Marauder.

He tried to count the number of men in the raiding force, but it was difficult. All the same he got the idea that the raiders had increased in number from when he had last seen them, and guessed that reinforcements had come to join them from south of the Border. Reinforcements? Tex found himself whistling as the word came into his head.

This was more like an army operation than the work of a thievin', rustlin' band. Plainly Pancho was operating in such strength that he could dare to go plundering and raiding far behind the Texas-Mexican border.

Tex stopped thinking in order to watch more closely. The Mexicans were going to have their fun with the prisoners. Tex saw the three prodded into a line with their backs to the Mexicans, and knew what it meant.

Raiders don't take prisoners. They can't; they'd only get in the way. Instead they were giving the bandits a chance to 'escape'.

'Some chance,' growled the cowboy to himself, watching, and curiously at this moment his sympathies were with Lem, Jud and Tucson, who a moment ago had been intent on killing him. Which shows how illogical is human nature.

But this was nothing short of murder, murder in the guise of sport. At a signal the three would be made to start running. When they were twenty or thirty yards away, the whole darned bunch of Mexicans would open up with every thing they'd got. In the unlikely event of any of the men being still alive the Mexicans would then ride them down.

They hadn't a chance, and Tex could see that the train-robbers knew it. Lem especially was arguing, pushing his captors off. He was shouting something across in the direction of Pancho the Mexican.

Suddenly his words seemed to have effect. Pancho came riding up very quickly, and began to talk to Lem. Then Tex gasped. Lem was pulling something out of his shirt pocket – the wallet. Senator Hooker's wallet, he was prepared to swear. Lem was drawing out papers and showing them to the Mexican leader.

One moment later the miracle was complete. To Tex's amazement the Mexican gave a peremptory command, and immediately horses were brought for the train-robbers; flabbergasted, the cowboy watched them mount – even saw their guns being given back to them.

'Now, what'n the tarnation's in that wallet?' he muttered. 'Must be pretty powerful medicine to save their lives like that.'

Then he stiffened as he saw the danger he was in. Lem was pointing back towards the dead horse. 'He's a-goin' to set the varmints on ter me,' he growled, and his rage rose. So near to the recent war between Texas and Mexico it seemed traitorous to employ Mexicans to hunt down another American – even an enemy.

Then his breath exploded in a long sigh. Pancho pointed to the declining sun and shook his head. Next minute the whole troop went riding eastward.

Tex let them disappear completely from sight, and then rose and dusted his pants.

'McQuade,' he said slowly, 'you're in one hellofa jam, ol' hoss. Now see'f you c'n get y'self outa this.'

He was horseless, in the heart of the broad strip of desert that runs on both sides of the Border. There'd be few homesteads this side of the rail track, and even if he knew where they were it was unlikely that he'd be able to make the distance afoot.

His only chance to get out of this desert, in fact, was to make for the rail track. He could see it from where he stood on this slight eminence – at any rate he could see the broken hills within which it lay; he could even see approximately where the water tank and spring was, where the hold-up had occurred such a little while ago.

But how far was it? Tex guessed it could be five or fifteen miles away. It didn't sound much, but the cowboy had no illusions. On this soft sand there'd be times when he'd be lucky if he could make a half mile in the hour. And he was a cowboy, and walking was foreign to him.

Tex went sliding down to where his dead horse lay, and got his war sack and water bottle, though there wasn't much water for such a long journey. If he lost sight of the broken hills and went off at a tangent, it would be just too bad.

He set off determinedly. Quarter of a mile down the arroya he sat down and took his boots off. They were worse than useless for this kind of work. Then for a time it was easier, until after a while thorns got through his skin and sent him limping.

Four hours later the sun set, and he seemed as far from the broken hills as ever. By this time his feet were bleeding from a dozen wounds, and they were so swollen that it was impossible for him to put his boots on now if he had wanted to.

Tex used precious water to clean his feet, then he bandaged them and curled up and went to sleep. It came cold after, as it does in this near-tropic region, and a pack of coyotes came and howled in a circle around him for most of the night. So the amount of sleep the cowboy got didn't amount to much. When light came strong enough to see his goal, he rose stiffly and began his painful march again.

He made the rail track on all fours, after noon that day, and the last hour was an experience that Tex wanted to forget and never would. The sun had got to his torn and blistered feet, and it had sent them swelling to astonishing proportions, and he'd run out of water, and the desert dryness left him as parched as a dried apple.

Then luck came his way. A freight train came wandering down the track, no more than an hour after he'd reached it; otherwise he'd have had a long crawl to the water tank – and that was many miles from the nearest habitation. A startled train crew saw a big, dust-covered hombre waving bandaged feet and fistfuls of dollars at them. The dollars were to let them see he was no rod-ridin' hobo, bent on a hitch. It was a non-scheduled train, with a good half day before anything else came along the track, so they halted for him. Tex looked up, grinning through cracked lips at them.

The driver, old and grey, exclaimed, 'What'n the hell, stranger?'

And the fireman, lanky and tobacco chewing, echoed. 'What'n the hell?'

Tex said, 'Look, I don't care ef that water is bilin', I'm a'goin' ter drink half on it.'

They hoisted him up on to the padded driver's-seat and attended to his feet while the old engine chugged steadily through the desert. Nobody bothered to look where they were going because, as the fireman said, 'This hyar train cain't get off'n the lines, can it? It knaws its way better'n we do, cowboy.'

It was after Tex had rubbed his face clean with a damp cloth, that the driver and fireman recognised him. 'Stranger,' began the driver, startled, 'you ain't—?'

'Elmer,' said the fireman, staring, 'it cain't be—'

The driver said, 'Look, son, you wouldn't kid an old fellar like me, I know. But tell me, ain't you the hombre that gave that Irish fellar the lickin' o' his life last Sat'day in Lozier.'

Tex said solemnly, 'Elmer, I wouldn't kid yer. Jes' look at these eyes o' mine and think how I could ha' got 'em.'

Then Tex became king. They'd have given him the train if he'd have asked for it. They'd had a stop over at Lozier that night, and they'd seen the fight. For them that scrap was the sweetest memory in years. They plied the cowboy with coffee, gave him their grub, and tied his feet up with their own bandanas. There was nothing too much for them to do for this fighting Texan.

'Gee whist,' said the lanky fireman, 'the way you come back. We thought you'd sure had it almost as soon as you got into the ring.'

They looked at him, one old boy and one not so young, hero-worshipping. From what they said even the champion's fight afterwards was an anti-climax. It had lacked the full bloodedness of the malice fight.

'Knaw what we did?' The fireman sprayed tobacco spit on to the passing desert. 'We kinda got tired o' them champs weavin' an' kissin' each other, so we up with our chairs an' slung 'em all in the ring. Reckon ef you show yore face in Lozier they'll make you mayor.'

They made up a bit of a bed for him, and he went off to sleep. But less than two hours later he was awake again. The train had stopped with a telescoping of cars, buffer against buffer for a quarter of a mile down the track. He felt that there was something wrong.

'What's the matter?' he said, sitting up among the wood. Silently they stood aside so that he could see.

They had stopped at what was an occasional halt. Here there was water, and the rail company had fixed sidings so that they could pick up herds from the northern holdings. A tiny village of maybe a couple of dozen buildings had grown up, as they always grew up where these sidings were fixed.

But what Tex now saw was no lazy, sunny, faded hamlet of straggly buildings.

He saw ruin and desolation, blackened timbers

and thin spirals of smoke still rising from them.

'Pancho!' he gasped. 'That's the varmint.' Yes, this would be the Mexican raider's handiwork. They all swung down on to the track, Tex ignoring his bandaged feet, and started searching. The crew from the brake van came running up ... But there wasn't a living soul. Corpses, many burnt beyond recognition of man. Plenty of corpses. But no one alive to tell the full story of what had happened.

'Reckon they attacked last night – maybe even after dark,' said Tex. 'Probably cut the telegraph wire, so that even now no one but ourselves knows of the tragedy. Then they must have shot and killed every livin' soul – looted the place, then set fire to it.'

They climbed back aboard the train, and started again. An hour later they saw a strong smoke spiral to the north, but it was too far off the track for them to stop and investigate. The driver said he thought there was a rancho up there, so they guessed that the Mexican raiders were still on the warpath. In the next hour they saw three other signs of blazing buildings.

The Border was in flames again, just as it had been during the time of the war; this Mexican and his small army was blazing a trail of destruction, the size of which was beyond reckoning. 'I don't understand it,' Tex said to himself. 'Ef it had been a bit of rustlin' an' lootin', or a bit o' burnin' by way of revenge, why that I could have understood. But this – this is organised destruction. Pancho's destroyin' fer the sake of destroyin'. That's not the way of a rustler, they don't stick their necks out fer nothin'.'

It was puzzling. He was trying to work it out, and

only vaguely heard what Elmer was saying to the fireman. The driver had looked at a gauge, and then started to apply the brakes.

'Stoppin'?' asked Tex. 'What is it this time?'

'Nothin',' said the driver, leaning out of the cab. 'Only water.'

Tex suddenly looked at the last smudge of smoke, maybe three miles north of them, the fire reflecting redly in it still. Then he dived for the control lever and shoved it full on, and the train began to pick up speed.

'What'n the—' began the driver, but Tex was leaning grimly out of the cab, looking to the approaching water tank.

'Keep down!' shouted the cowboy, and simultaneously drew with one hand. Elmer went down, but not before he'd seen the sombreroes and masked faces hard by the side of the water tank. Then a screaming shower of lead spanged on to the steel plating of the engine – the fireman found the shovel revolving in his hand as it caught a ricocheting bullet.

CHAPTER SEVEN

THEY'RE NOT RUSTLERS!

They were picking up speed well, however, and the horsemen who galloped to try and clamber aboard the moving freight cars found that a slow freight train moves far faster than they'd thought.

Tex blazed away, but rocking as they were he didn't think he caused much damage. When he saw that the pursuit had given up the attempt to board them, he turned and reloaded and grinned at his companions.

'You know somep'n,' he said, 'that was pure hunch an' it came off. I heard you say you were stoppin' fer water, an' I remember stopping fer water on a train only last week. I remembered being held up – an' suddenly I remembered that the same gang that held up the train was now ridin' with them blamed Mexes. So I decided maybe the ol' train wasn't so thirsty an' might make a few more miles ter the next water hole.'

The old driver was shaken. 'It's a durned good job you did, cowboy. Them Mexes was sure intendin' to hold up the freight train. Guess they'd have blown up Old Faithful an' set fire to the cars, but fer you. The pesky, destroyin' Mexican varmints!'

'An' more than Mexes,' said Tex quietly. 'You saw them masked hombres – two of them? Jes' two galoots wearin' masks?' They nodded. 'Wal, them two was my old' pals, Lem 'n Jud Cole, I guess. Them renegades is ridin an' lootin' an' destroyin' along with the Mexes. You can understand the Mexes doin' it, to some extent but not fer Americans ter join 'em in their dirty work.'

They sped on for a few more miles, silent as they thought of the traitors. Then Tex said, 'Thar's a town not far from here, called Old Bull Crossing. It's too big to be attacked by Pancho, so I reckon they'll skirt it an' go raidin' the smaller places. But mebbe this hyar town don't know 'bout Pancho an' his raids, so we'd better warn 'em. They c'n telegraph up an' down the line, and can send riders out to warn the smaller places and ranches. Mebbe they c'n get some Texas Rangers sent up, too.'

The town was blissfully ignorant of the fiery trail that had been lighted all along the Border, and at first they didn't seem to believe Tex or the train crew when they spoke of armed Mexican raiders several hundred strong. Then Tex pointed back the way they had come, to where a distant smoke pillar spiralled into the sky ... and even more distantly, where there were two similar smoke stacks.

Then he asked, 'What d'yer think them are, sher'ff? Cig'ret smokers?'

That did it. The small cow-town became a

madhouse of armed posses dashing out by every trail to give warning to isolated ranchos and townships. But the freight train had only time to take on water before passing on.

They reached Lozier in the early hours of the morning, and found it curiously wide awake. There were lots of people in the streets; the news of the latest Border raids had come through very late, and now in their different ways the citizens of Lozier were up and taking action.

But Tex simply rolled into the train-crew's dosshouse, along with the driver, fireman and brake-van crew, and went fast asleep. He'd had enough. On the job he didn't get time to recover from one murderous thrashing before fresh injuries came to take their place. He slept – he was still sleeping at mid-day. Then the train crew woke him, because they had to go on, and they wanted to shake his hand again. Tex thought humorously, 'Ef every fellar that saw that fight wants ter shake my hand, I'm goin' ter have my arm torn right out of its socket.'

Elmer fetched him some soft Mexican sandals for his feet, and thus attired the cowboy was able to limp round to the nearest livery stable. Five minutes later it didn't matter if his feet were in a mess – he'd got his legs round horseflesh, and if anyone got sore feet it would be his mount, not him.

Then he went round to the Hotel Mexicana to see the senator. That's why he had come to Lozier, so he told himself – to tell the Senator he could forget about his papers. Now he didn't think there was a possible chance that anyone could ever recover them. He certainly wasn't going to try. To date it had cost him two horses. True, one he'd 'borrowed', but horses were mighty heavy on the bank-roll, and he couldn't afford to spend the senator's dollars that way much more. Anyway, surrounded by an army of Mexicans, Tex didn't think there was a chance of getting at the bandit brothers again.

They told him that the senator was out but was expected back shortly.

So Tex went to look for Lavender Grey, and realised that that was the real reason for his quick return to Lozier – it had nothing to do with the senator!

He found her very quickly. She made no bones about it, she was looking for him, too.

'Tex!' she called, and the cowboy heard her cry and looked across the stream of buggies and horse-flesh that made the thriving Border capital a place to talk about on lonely ranchos. He saw her, and whipped his new mount to her side.

She was on the high seat of the buggy; whoever had come in with her was in the general store. She smiled up at him, and there was welcome all over her good-looking, friendly face. She liked Tex, and wasn't bothered about hiding her feelings; Miss Lavender Grey was a forthright young person, impatient with deception and the usual feminine arch-nesses.

'Lavender,' almost shouted Tex in delight, and she didn't seem to notice the omission of the usual 'Miss' or 'Ma'am', so he never used those terms to her again, except in fun.

'Tex!' Her voice jumped a note with concern. 'Your face again, and – and your feet.' She could see the bandages under the open-work sandals. 'What have you been up to, cowboy?'

'Got mixed up with them blamed train-robbers,' he said in disgust. 'Didn't get nowhere. Killed one, I reckon – the grinnin' fellar they called Pinky – and bust the shoulder of another. That was all.'

'That was all? Just killed one hombre and winged another. My, my, cowboy, you'll have to do better than that. Guess they'll be callin' you cissie soon.'

Tex blinked, then saw she was dead-panning. 'Aw, shucks,' he grinned awkwardly, 'what I mean is, with a bit of luck I might ha' nailed them galoots an' got yore locket back. But ... I guess I never expected a hombre to use a pardner to draw the fire, like Lem did with Pinky. That's somep'n I ain't never heerd of afore, even among scallywaggin' train-robbers.'

'Reckon you'd better start from the beginnin', Tex, you old war-horse,' said the girl dryly. He looked at the store. 'That's all right,' she assured him. 'It's not Pop ridin' herd over me today; it's Sam, the cook, an' I can take care o' him. Pop was sending him into Lozier to stock up with ammunition against these pesky Mexican raiders, so I thought I'd come along an' see what you were doing.'

Tex felt a glow suffuse his body. He'd made more than first base with Lavender Grey, it seemed, and the thought was exhilarating. He told her of his adventures, and her eyes widened steadily as laconically he told of his fight and the trailing of Irish – then of his fight and the capture of the three bandits by the Mexicans.

He had dismounted by this time, and was standing on the busy sidewalk, his right foot resting on the spokes of the front near-side wheel of the buggy. Thoughtfully he looked into the dust and shook his head.

'It sure beats me,' he said. 'One minute them varmints is prisoners an' about to have a race agen lead, next thing, they're ridin' with them Mexicans, takin' part in their raids. What magic was there in that wallet, I keep askin' myself?'

Lavender frowned, too. 'That's what Pop keeps sayin',' she said. 'He says he can understand rustlin', but these Mexes aren't rustlers. They're just doing as much damage as they can, and they're doing it in such a way as to get all Texas hoppin' mad, which they've done.'

'So I've noticed,' grinned Tex. 'Some o' the aforesaid citizens of Texas were lighting out on hosses aroun' three o'clock this mornin'.'

'They were?' – quickly. 'Why, Tex? Where were they goin'?'

'Looked mighty like a raidin' party to me,' said Tex. 'Trouble was, I was too darned tired to take much interest. Reckon they was goin' on a retal – retalia—'

'Retaliatory raid?'

'As you say,' agreed Tex agreeably. 'What c'n you expect? Them Mexes can't be allowed to burn up Texas an' get away with it, can they?'

'I don't know, Tex.' Lavender surprised him by shaking her head slowly. 'Perhaps it's not all as simple as it seems to you right now. I mean, what good will retaliatory raids do? That'll make other Mexicans mad against Texas, and there'll be more raiders over the Border.'

'Then,' said Tex grimly, 'we'll get just that bit madder an' by glory ther'll be no Mexes left.'

Lavender looked down at him, her face mockingly sorrowful. 'Mr McQuade,' she said, shaking her head, 'when it comes to a fight, you're my man every

91

time, but when it comes to elementary logic—'

'What?' said Tex suspiciously.

'All right, cowboy, when it comes to brainwork, you start right back with the dogies.'

'That,' said Tex, shoving back his hat, 'is fightin' talk. Do we start now, or wait until—' His voice trailed off in horror at what he was about to say.

'What were you going to say?' asked Lavender, and there was butter melting in her pretty mouth.

'Aw, nuthin',' grinned Tex awkwardly.

'Nuthin'?' she repeated, and her voice was soft. 'You weren't by any chance trying to say, "Do we start fightin' now – or wait until we get married?" Was that it, Tex McQuade?'

She was laughing at him. A chit of a girl, performing the feminine equivalent of laughing her head off. Tex thought, 'This is some gal. She can sass you, an' she can hold her own agen you. She's a tough little lass, an' she's a mighty fine sense of humour.' She was the kind of girl he'd thought about, but hadn't suspected existed.

Sam the cook came out just then, and wondered what'n the hades they were howlin' their heads off at. Some durn' joke o' their own. He was in time to hear Tex say, 'Wal, Lavender Grey, you ain't give me an answer, so quit hidin' behind a smile.'

'Never did object to a fight at any time,' she said coolly. 'By your face, it looks mighty easy to get through your guard, cowboy.'

Tex grinned with delight at the way she was kidding him. And it emboldened him to ask, softly, 'An the other part – gettin' married – how long might that be away, d'you reckon?'

She didn't blush and simper and go all coy. She

just laughed down into his face and said, 'Sonny boy, if you go on usin' your face as a doormat for other people's feet, reckon the answer will be never. My, you should see yourself in a mirror!'

'I have,' said Tex meekly, but his heart was bounding. She didn't mean a word of what she said; instinctively he knew that Tex McQuade was a right nice an' appealing hombre, so far as Lavender Grey was concerned, and he was satisfied.

Sam said, darkly, 'What's this talk 'bout marryin', Miss Lavender? Don't you let your paw ketch you with them thoughts.' He hoisted a case of ammunition on to the already crowded buckboard, and stiffly climbed into the driving seat.

'We'd better say good-bye,' smiled Lavender. 'Now don't get hurt, Tex, will you? Not on my account any way.' She meant that. 'And Tex, don't you go joinin' any guerillas goin' out to burn up Mexico.'

'But that's the only thing we can do' protested Tex. 'We ain't gonna let no blamed Mexes get away with this.'

'Cowboy,' said Lavender offensively, 'I don't know what keeps your ears apart, but it isn't brains. Don't you see, Tex, that's just what someone is wanting you all to do.'

'What?' said Tex, belligerently. He was out of his depth.

'Why, start the war all over again.'

'But, why?' – bewildered.

'Because some people make money out of wars. Now, you go out and find out who's behind all this and rope him in and – and—'

'And what'll you do?' grinned Tex.

Lavender Grey looked down at him, a little smile

playing at the corner of her mouth. Then she patted his shoulder consolingly and said, teasingly, 'I don't know, cowboy, I just got to fix you with a new face before I c'n think what's best for you.'

Then Sam got tired and whipped up the hosses, and Tex was left standing on the pavement, his hat waving deliriously after the girl. 'Hoss,' he said, when she'd turned the corner, 'I could kiss you!' And what's more he did, right there and then. He grabbed the surprised animal by the ears and gave it a loud smack between the eyes.

Then he saw a frowsty old stumblebum watching him, and heard the old hobo say, "Tain't the same cowboy. Not 'nless the gal oughta start ter shave.'

Tex hadn't anything else to do but get his feet better in the next few hours. He had no plans, but in his heart he knew that he was going to hang around Lozier for a while yet until he could adjust Lavender Grey into or out of his life. He'd go around to see the senator tomorrow and tell him there wasn't any future in going after the train-robbers while they were sitting in the middle of an army of Mexes. Then he'd go find a job. Maybe it would be politic not to get one on the Two-by-Two.

If you're young and healthy, you soon recover from injury. Next morning the swelling had considerably diminished on his feet, and he thought that in another day he'd be able to get his boots on.

He awoke from a beautiful dream in which Jud and Lem were marrying and fighting all the time, and the parson was (of all people!) Senator Claude C. Hooker. And every now and then both the bride and groom would turn on the senator and shoot a few holes in him.

Waking, the cowboy wasn't so sure that his dream had finished, because the noise out in the street was close unto bedlam. He dressed in a hurry and went out of the boarding house. People were standing around reading a special edition of the Lozier paper. Tex found he'd come down without his money, but someone gave him a copy and he returned to his room to read it.

The main item of news was about the Pancho raiders. The report said that the raiding force appeared to have grown, and it now numbered between three and four hundred. Reports were coming in that small groups of Mexicans were slipping over the Border to join the triumphant raiders. The significance of this latter item was that these parties knew where to meet up with the main force, which suggested considerable preconcerted planning.

That was the main theme on the front page. 'Has Mexico started the war again?' the headlines asked. 'Was this just a way of getting a strong force into Texas before war proper was joined?' the editorial suggested.

Reports were not too exact about the extent of the raiding forces depredations, said the paper, because Pancho appeared to have destroyed most of the telegraph wires west along the rail track and for thirty or forty miles inland. It was known, however, that late the previous day he had attacked a small township less than forty miles west of Lozier.

'Getting nearer,' thought Tex, disturbingly near.

So thought Lozier. When Tex went out to get something to eat, the streets were beginning to get uncomfortably packed. People were riding in with their womenfolk from the neighbouring ranchos, and there was a lot of shouting and bad temper in consequence, and a lot of tears from the ladies. It made Tex's head whirl, all those nervous, prancing horses, all those crazy buggies and high-wheeled wagons getting locked and nearly spilling and everyone cracking whips and shouting and bawling and telling the other fellow off.

Then he found a group of people attending a meeting down by where the Orleans Tavern stood. He saw that all had guns and looked mighty serious, so he joined in at the back.

There was a big *hombre* shouting his head off. He didn't look a cowman, and he had the pale face you see up in Yankee-land. But he could talk.

'Who's this galoot?' Tex whispered to a man carrying a rifle. But the man shook his head.

'Ain't never seen him afore,' he said, and seemed suddenly surprised at the thought. Then he straightened and remarked, fiercely, 'All the same, this is one guy that's got his head screwed on right good an' watertight. He's talkin' sense, plenty sense.'

Talking? He seemed to be asking questions, thought Tex, and the way he put them sounded so scornful it made you shift in your boots uneasily.

'You satisfied?' the fellar kept saying. 'Look, them Mexes is just playin' ring-a-roses up there. They're doing just as they like – shooting, killing, burning, destroying. That's true, ain't it?'

A loud growl went up from the crowd.

'Well, what's the government doing about it? Nothing gents, I guess they're doing nothing. All they can say is, "Keep calm, we're going to do something". But what can they do? Can they stop Pancho and his gang before they've burned up the Border? No, I tell you. It doesn't matter how many men are sent out, Pancho has horses just as fast and he'll keep one jump ahead. And if the pursuit gets too close, why I reckon he'll just slip over the Border and thumb his nose at his pursuers.'

That angered the crowd, and they shouted disapproval, not of the speaker but of the frustrating situation.

'That wouldn't be so bad,' went on the speaker, 'if we could ride into Mexico after the vermin. But do you think the government will let us? No, sir. They'd bleat that that was a violation of the peace treaty with Mexico. Pancho knows that, he's bankin' on it. He knows he's safe across the Border, and he knows he can bob back as often as he likes, burnin' an' killin'. Just as often as he likes.'

He paused and looked round the crowd, and then shouted. 'Unless we take the war into our own hands!'

Tex scuffled the dirt with his sandal, and then turned and limped away. He was disturbed. He knew that he would have stayed with that crowd and shouted with them, but for the fact that Lavender had sown a seed of suspicion in his mind the previous day. But for those words of hers he would never have given a thought to the higher implications of war and the profit to be derived therefrom.

Now, this pale-faced Yankee kinda fellar – he seemed to be whipping up the crowd into some sort of action. Was he going to make anything out of developing a war? Because even Tex could see that war wasn't far away, and if this scrap was allowed to develop, it could restart hostilities between the two countries.

He drifted away, puzzling, head bent in thought. After a little while he noticed that a pair of riding boots were keeping pace with him, one yard to his right. Then he realised that another pair of riding boots were pacing in step to his left.

He stopped abruptly and the boots stopped, too. His head jerked up, and he found himself looking into two of the toughest faces he'd seen in a long time.

'It's him,' he heard one of the men say, and then Tex started to go for his guns.

CHAPTER EIGHT

AN END TO A RENEGADE

They both looked about two yards wide, those *hombres* and Tex wasn't taking chances. His guns came into his hands as if they'd been cold and wanted warming, and their blue noses were turned frigidly towards the big *hombres*.

Tex said, icily, 'Sure it's me. It's been me fer a long time. More, I intend goin' on being me for the next forty-five years.'

One of the galoots nodded approvingly. 'Reckon you might make it, McQuade, at that. Yore draw sure is a tribute to plenty homework.'

Tex was puzzled. Back of their dead pan countenances he felt there was a glint of humour lurking. One sighed and said, 'Pity, Dirk, we gotta put this boy in jail ain't it?'

Dirk gave a sigh like the tide going out and said, 'Sure is, Alec. Reckon we gotta do it.'

'Jail?' rapped Tex. 'I don't get it, pardners.'

'No?' Alec lifted eyebrows that were quite defi-
nitely humorous now. 'Sure you know it's illegal to
draw down on the Texas Rangers.'

'Rangers?' said Tex, shoving back his guns. 'You
these hyar new Rangers?'

'We sure are.' The Texas Rangers had been formed
to keep order on the frontier following the recent
war. As yet they were a little-known force, all tough,
hard-bitten volunteers, but few in number.

'We want a word with you, McQuade,' said Alex. 'I
recognised you when you came into the crowd. You
kinda tidied up that red-headed fellar at the arena,
las' Sat'day, didn't you?'

'He did his share o' tidying, too,' grinned the
cowboy.

'Looks like it,' said Alex dryly. 'Look, son, I think
you could do us Rangers a powerful lot of good.'

'Me? How?' That was a shaker to the cowboy.
How'n the Hades could they expect him to be of any
help to the Rangers, short of enlisting, which he
wasn't goin' ter do, no, sir!

'Before I tell you, just one question.' The Rangers
were watching him keenly. 'This fellow you've been
a-hearin' spielin' back there – what d'yer think o' his
sentiments, pardner?'

Tex was honest. 'I reckon but fer one thing I'd be
shoutin' "Hear, hear", like the rest of the folk right
now.'

'An' what was that one thing?'

'A gal I know, she said, "Watch out fer *hombres*
who will try n' develop this trouble an' make money
outa it". Something like that she said, anyway.'

'That gal,' said Alex, 'has brains. She may not be
pretty, but she's got a mite of stuffing inside her skull.'

'That gal,' said Tex coldly, 'is so durned pretty that I'll smack any man's ears right bang together if he says thar's another gal in the world like her.'

'Reckon I did hyar someone say some'pn detrimental about yore gal at that,' said the Ranger, dead-panning again.

'An' who was that?'

'Pancho, the Mexican.'

'Then I'll go out right now an' kill the varmint.'

'That,' said Alec, 'is why we came to talk to yer,' and then all three stopped and laughed at each other. They went into a bar that shouldn't have been open because the Governor had said that liquor might inflame the populace at this time. But some saloonkeepers couldn't read the Order, and others were too busy serving drink to pay any attention to it, anyway.

'Now, what's it all about?' asked Tex, fingering his glass. Captain Alec Gilray, officer commanding the Lozier company of Texas Rangers, told him.

'We're up against something, something big. This Pancho business had promoted a very ticklish situation – it doesn't need much to restart the war between the United States and Mexico. Worse, it almost seems as though some powerful interests are doin' their darndest to get us at each other's throats again.'

'Interests?' queried Tex.

Captain Gilray nodded. 'We don't know who they are or what they are up to, but all this Pancho affair looks like some deliberate and well-planned scheme to foment the maximum amount of trouble. Whoever's behind it must be big.'

'If it's as big as all this,' said Tex dryly, 'why this

interest in a cowpoke by the name of McQuade?'

'You're a pretty popular fellar, Tex, that's why we're interested in you. The crowd loves a fighter, and you gave 'em their money's worth at the arena last week. They won't forget that. They'll take notice of you. If you tell 'em to be good boys an' do as the Governor tells 'em, they'll take heed of what yore sayin'.'

Tex characteristically shoved his hat to the back of his head and said, 'I'm way out o' my depth, pardners. I don't even know what the Governor's been sayin', so how can I tell 'em to follow his advice?'

'The Governor's saying, keep calm. Leave it to us to handle this affair.'

'So I heard at that meeting.' Tex nodded. 'An' the crowd didn't seem ter think much o' the advice. Seemed ter reckon it amounted ter jes' so much soft soap.'

'Well, Tex, you'd be doin' Texas a mighty fine favour if you could persuade the crowd that what the Governor says ain't soft soap.'

'You gotta convince me first,' said the cowboy, shrewdly. 'You see, captain, I seen these Pancho *hombres* at work. I seen a li'l town left so high by them varmints – all black an' smokin' and not a human being left ter say what it felt like to be roasted. They're killers, captain an' I don't like that sort of killin'. My instinct is ter go and do somethin' about it, not jes' sit and be calm.'

'Well, darn yer,' exploded the Ranger captain, 'you can do something about it, you an' all the Lozier fireeaters. We're not at war, so we can't conscript the men we want, an' we want a lot, Tex, a mighty lot. So we gotta try an' talk you squareheads into volunteering ter help us, an' the trouble is there are so many mischief-makers shootin' their heads off that they cannot hear us.'

'They don't want to,' said Dirk Humphrys in disgust. 'Them blamed Yankee word-speilers are inflaming the crowd so that they won't listen to reason. It won't do any good to dash off into Mexico and burn a few towns by way of revenge. What we've got to do it to stop Pancho from killin' and destroying' any more. We gotta catch him an' hand him over to the authorities to be properly taken care of. That's the only way to stop his Border trouble. Startin' a war with Mexico won't do it.'

'But how in the Hades can you catch Pancho?' snapped Tex. 'I agree with you as far as you've gone, but I don't see how you can lay hands on that Mexican quicksilver. It's as that Yankee fellar said – Pancho's well mounted, an' he can keep ahead of any pursuit. An' when he gets tired o' run-in', over the Border he'll go an' he and all his men will just quietly disperse to their villages until they feel like another raid. That ain't exactly an encouragin' proposition.'

'No, but it's one we've got to tackle, anyway. What's more, if we could get Lozier men to follow us, 'stead o' dashin' off into Mexico at night, we could finish this Pancho fellar in a matter o' days, or at the most weeks.'

'You could?' That was interesting; it made the prospect brighter.

'Sure.' The captain looked round, as if to make sure he wasn't being overheard. 'Now, Tex, you look like a square-shooter ter me, so I'm gonna tell you what the Governor's plan is. You must promise that under no circumstances will you talk about it to anyone.'

'I promise.'

'The Governor's an old Injun' fighter, as you know. He's a shrewd old man, an' he's got a plan which he calls a "probin' finger". The idea is that we send posses of ten men at fifteen minute intervals west along the Border. That means that one day after we start the plan, we'll have round about sixty groups of men strung along he frontier. Guess we would have a "finger" probing seventy, eighty or more miles in length between Pancho and his own country.

'Wal, at sunrise on the second day, all these posses will turn an' ride north. Somewhere, sometime, some posse or other's bound to meet up with the Pancho gang. As soon as the first posse fires a warning, every other posse will close in. The Governor's supplying Winchesters, and that should give us a powerful advantage. Reckon that way we can beat the hide off Pancho by the time everyone's standin' bleatin' about doin' something in Lozier.'

'Sure, I see that,' drawled Tex, toying with his glass. 'But what'n the heck are you tellin' me this for? What do you want me to do?'

Gilray said, 'Go out an' persuade four or five hundred men to volunteer their services for the Rangers.'

Tex choked and put down his glass. 'But why me?'

'Because most o' the fightin' men o' Lozier know you. Ef you talk to 'em, they'll join – mebbe. You're our only hope, Tex. We can't, obviously, go around tellin' everyone what the Governor's plan is, an' it's difficult persuading a man to join you if he thinks you are without plans. We've tried, an' see how far we've got. Nowhere. And time's racin' by. Tex, the Governor's goin' to address a big meeting outside Government House this afternoon. He's goin' ter have a rough time. We want you to go and give him your support. After the way you licked the big red-head, they'll respect you and listen to you, and that, mebbe, 'll give the Governor a chance to talk 'em over. What say, Tex?'

Tex thought of Lavender Grey and downed his glass. He said, 'I can but try. I'll be there. Now I'm goin' ter see my late boss,' and with that they walked out.

The meeting was called for shortly after noon, and what happened there is now largely history — history of the Border at any rate. The Governor came out on top of the broad steps before the big doors of Government House, but an incensed mob wouldn't listen to him. He stood there, a white-haired old man; below him swayed a sea of mutinous faces — they say that ten thousand packed Government Square that afternoon, and everyone was seemingly against the Governor.

People said that the Governor was supine; they said he was weak in the face of their late enemy, Mexico. They said that he was bluffing; he had no plan of action, and was only pretending he had.

So when the old Governor raised his hand for quiet, a howl of execration rose from those ten thousand people, drowning the sound of his voice. Time after time he tried to speak, and every time he was howled down.

Then someone climbed upon the balustrade and began to address the citizens of Lozier. This time the audience was content to listen — more than that, it roared its approval at the course of action that the Yankee voice as advocating.

'Why chase the Mexican will-o'-the-wisp over half of Texas, when Mexico's a few hundred yards from us right now? Why don't we go out, just as some good citizens went out last night, and teach these goddam'd Mexes that they can't come robbin' an' burnin' with impunity this side of the Border? If we give 'em a taste o' their own medicine, they'll soon draw their horns in!'

A mighty roar swelled from the crowd at that. This was fighting talk; this was the sort of talk they wanted to hear.

'For every ranch they've destroyed, let's go an' burn two Mexican's. For every town they've beaten up, let's destroy two o' theirs. And for every Texan they've killed let's kill two Mexes!'

Now the roar rose to a chorus that was like the baying of wolves when they sense a kill. These Texans had suffered; many had lost their ranchos, their cattle – and often some members of their family. Revenge was sweet to contemplate and the Yankee was whipping them into a mood so ugly they were deaf to reason and blind to anything beyond the tip of their noses.

The old Governor's lined face seemed to go grey as he heard the crowd. It wasn't with personal fear; the old man was afraid of nothing that walked on two or four legs. But he was seeing in a moment his work, and the work of others on both sides of the Border, destroyed in a few days by the irresponsible if not unscrupulous activities of a small number of scheming men. He knew that if the citizens of Lozier defied international law and the recent peace treaty made between the Border countries; if they went en masse, killing and destroying – then it would reopen war between the countries, and neither could afford to continue the bitter struggle.

'If only I could do something,' he whispered to himself. 'If only they would listen to me!' But they would not. Again and again he tried to make himself heard, but each time he did so a howl went up from the nearby section of the crowd, drowning his words.

Even his good friend, Senator Claude C. Hooker, was denied speech. He tried his best, but in the end he, too, had to give in. No single voice could possibly compete against that bitter, angry chorus.

'I've done my best, Jim,' he said to the Governor. 'But they're off their heads. They won't listen to reason.'

'Sure you've done your best,' said the Governor. 'No one could have done better. I'm afraid the situation is completely out of hand now. Reckon the best thing for me to do is resign – I've failed, badly.'

It seemed as though he had failed. The Yankee orator was whipping the audience into a white hot fury. Every sentence was punctuated with a roar from the crowd, and it surged violently, uncontrollably, as passions rose and demanded an outlet for its energy. The handful of Rangers and military was completely helpless in the face of such an overwhelming mob.

Down by where the Governor was standing, two Rangers scanned the hostile crowd. One said, 'He's failed us, Dirk. I thought I could rely on that *hombre's* promise, but it seems he's changed his mind.'

'Too bad,' said Dirk Humphrys. 'But I guess even

the fightin' cowboy wouldn't get anywhere with this raving mob. It's just as well he got cold feet, for I guess that's why he vamoosed. They wouldn't'a listened to him, Alec.'

'But he could have tried,' said the Ranger captain, shortly. 'We've always got to try, for even long shots come off occasionally.'

One came off that afternoon. It was when the situation was passing right out of hand; when the mob was about to depart for their horses and go blazing into Mexican territory. When, so it seemed to the old Governor of Texas, that everything was lost.

Suddenly a lone figure came striding out from the back of the building, along the high walk towards the head of the of the steps. He was a big, rangy cowboy, without hat and wearing sandals in place of the usual cowboy boots.

But what secured the crowd's attention, what made them cease their howling so that suddenly there was a deathly quiet over the square, was the fact that over the big cowboy's shoulder lay a figure ominously limp and still.

The cowboy strode to the top of the steps, then casually dropped his burden so that it rolled two or three steps down. Then he stood and faced the silent mob, his legs firmly astride, his hands on his thighs ... his head set back on his shoulders as if in contemptuous challenge of the whole ten thousand.

Suddenly the cowboy spoke, his voice harsh but carrying to all that silent crowd.

'He's dead,' he said, pointing to the still huddle of clothes and flesh at his feet. Then his voice rose a little.

'I jes' killed him.'

He paused. Then out came the challenge.

'An' I reckon thar's a few more *hombres* in this crowd that I'll be killin' before the day's out, an' one's that goddam'd Yankee agitator that's stirrin' up mischief an' makin' you bigger fools than the good Lord intended you to be!'

It was then that a whisper started and went right through the crowd. The cowboy saw faces turning, and it seemed to him it was like a field of corn bending before a breeze ... the whisper began a murmur that rose into a gentle roar.

'It's the fightin' cowboy,' they told each other. 'That Tex McQuade that licked the hide off'n that other Irish fellar on Sat'day. Be glory, an' what a scrapper! What a fight!'

It was Tex McQuade. Tex – hopping, raging, burning mad. Tex, ready to take on the whole darned town of Lozier so outraged was he just at that moment.

CHAPTER NINE

THE RANGERS NEED YOU!

Tex didn't do it consciously. He was no actor, but his entry on to that scene was dramatic. Probably there was no other way in which he could have quietened that mob as he did and secure their absorbing interest.

But he secured the crowd's attention all right. More, because he pitched into them, because he had the temerity to stand and cuss them, they loved him for it. That's the way it is – flatter a crowd and they'll jeer; tell 'em they're goddarned, four-flushing palookas and it will delight them.

And Tex was mad. The amazed Governor and his party watched the big cowboy storm to and fro along the head of the steps, fists clenched and swinging as if he would take on every mother's son in the square.

'You know who this fellar is?' Tex shouted, pointing again to the body. 'His name's Judson, Judson Cole. He was a no-good, thievin', rustlin', train-

110

robbin' varmint, but I reckon I don't hold that too much agen him.

'What I do hold agen him – an' it's the reason why I drilled him – is that he was a renegade to his own kind. You know what this good American did? To save his own skin he joined up with the Pancho gang. He went shootin', robbin' an' burnin' Texans an' Texans' property. I know, I saw him doin' it. Death was too good for him, but I saw he got his!'

A savage roar went up from the crowd. They approved of what the cowboy had done, approved and wanted more. The big cowboy held up his hand, and they fell silent. He was still mad, and now he attacked the crowd.

'I don't see what you've got to shout about,' he taunted. 'This Cole fellar was a rogue, but you – why, yore a passel o' fools!' For the space of two minutes he whiplashed the bewildered crowd, calling them every insulting name he could lay tongue to. If he hadn't been popular with them, they would never have suffered it, but a crowd respects a fighting man and Tex had certainly proved himself a fighter.

But at length a cracked old voice raised in protest from the crowd. 'Hey, cowboy, what'n the tarnation hev we done wrong?'

'Wrong?' hurled back Tex. 'Haven't you been listening to another renegade all mornin' an' this afternoon? That Yankee fellar that's been doin' his darndest to get you to violate Mexican territory is a far more dangerous man that this renegade hyar. Yer darn fools, what good would it do ter go an' shoot up half o' Mexico? Wouldn't it be better ter go out an' stop Pancho from killin' any more Texans? Wouldn't it be better ter go out an' put an end to his games, 'stead of startin' a few more fires south o' the border?'

The crowd buzzed, taken aback by the vehemence of his attack. The aged Governor let his face crack into a great grin. 'What a boy!' he chuckled. 'Goldarn it, that boy's just a natural orator and he don't know it!'

'Sure,' said Tex, 'I know what they've bin tellin' yer. They've bin sayin' that it's impossible ter catch Pancho. They've bin sayin' that the Governor's got no plan to match the Mex.

'Wal, I know he has. An' it's a good plan. Ef four or five hundred o' you noisy *hombres* would volunteer fer the Rangers, Pancho could be wiped out within a few days – fer certain!'

'Why doesn't he tell us the plan?' someone shouted.

'An' have some renegade ride out an' warn Pancho?' asked Tex, witheringly. 'The only way to deal with Pancho is not to let him know what you intend ter do. That's common sav, ain't it?'

A murmur of approval went up from the crowd. Tex hadn't won them over yet, but he'd got them thinking a little and that was something.

'Folks,' said Tex, 'I made Judson talk afore he died. I told him that unless he gave me the truth I'd see he died – slowly. I guess he didn't want ter die – slowly. So he talked.

'Thar's some mighty powerful people tryin' ter make suckers outa Lozier people. They aim ter get Mexico and Texas at war agen, an' they planned ter use you people ter start the war off.

'Pancho's in their pay!' A fierce murmur from the crowd. 'That's the truth I'm tellin' yer. Pancho's no

112

Border rustler; he's bin paid ter terrorise the Border and make Texas hostile towards Mexico agen. An' there are people here in Lozier who are being paid ter get you Lozier folks takin' the war into Mexico – so's these powerful people c'n make nice fat profits outa the war.'

The roar that went up at that was as ferocious as any that had been heard there that day. No man likes to think he's been led by the nose, not even when everyone else has been similarly led. In a few minutes Tex had turned them from one plan of action to a plan diametrically opposite.

Tex waved for them to quieten. When the murmur had subsided, the cowboy snarled, 'I don't like traitors, an' I don't like renegades. An' I know the names o' some o' the people who are tryin' ter make trouble.

'The first is a professional agitator from New York named Stayer, Sid Stayer. Reckon that might be you up thar, huh?' The Yankee started to address the crowd again, but was howled down. 'The Rangers thought he might be doin' a paid job but they hadn't any proof. Reckon I got it fer them,' said Tex. ' 'Cordin' to the law, Stayer should be handed over—'

But the crowd howled, 'Lynch the renegade!' and Stayer was suddenly surrounded. He tried to go for his gun, but someone beat him to it ...

And Stayer had made his last act of mischief that afternoon, his last forever.

Tex quietened them again. "There are other names, but I didn't get the name I wanted most of all – the name of the man or men behind these Border raiders an' agitators. He suddenly dived fer my gun, an' regretfully I had ter perferate the gent. I don't know the ringleader o' these varmints, but I think I

113

know where I can get the information. You bet I'm goin' ter get it, an' when I do I'll hang the pizenous reptile from the highest cottonwood!'

That's what Tex told the crowd, and it was nearly correct. What he didn't tell them was that he had his suspicions, but daren't voice them because the man he suspected was too big and could get away with it. But he knew where he could get proof, and if it was the last thing he did, he was going to nail the *hombre* who had started all the killing and destruction along the Border.

Just now he had other work to do. Captain Alex Gilray had mounted the steps and was intently watching him. Tex knew what was in the Ranger's mind, and for a second he grinned down at Gilray. 'You're wantin' them four or five hundred men, captain, huh? Betcha I get 'em now!'

Captain Gilray took one look at the grinning, fighting face above him, glanced for a second at the raging, angry crowd and his voice exulted. 'Bet you will, cowboy,' he grinned back. 'Bet you could get 'em to eat out o' your hand if you asked 'em to!'

Tex made his last throw, gambling all to win, though now he had little doubt. 'Pardners,' he called, 'I'm a-goin' ter volunteer to help the Rangers round up the Pancho raiders. Reckon it'll be a week's job only, ef four or five hundred active, well-mounted *hombres* volunteer. Captain Gilray don't want loud-mouths an' cripples, he wants men. Let's see if there are any among you!'

Perhaps it was that little touch of insult that turned the scale. Captain Gilray didn't want cripples; well, they weren't cripples – they were men an' a-ra'rin' ter prove it!

Captain Gilray was able to take his pick that afternoon, there were so many volunteers that he could afford to eject the services of many stout-hearted but physically unfit men. The Rangers needed tough, seasoned Border fighters for this campaign, and Lozier supplied all that he asked for.

While the men were being drafted and taken away to collect Winchesters, ammunition and food, Tex went over to where the Governor was standing. The old man rose as he strode up, his face suffused with pleasure and gratitude.

'Son,' he said, 'that was magnificent. All Texas is in your debt for what you have just done.'

'Shucks,' grinned Tex, 'reckon you c'n do anythin' if you're plenty mad, an' I sure was blazin' over what Jud told me.'

'Any time you want to become Governor,' said the old man dryly, 'it seems you only need to get plenty mad, then!'

But the big cowboy was looking beyond him, looking into the uncertain eyes of the paunchy, pink and perspiring Senator Claude C. Hooker. The Governor turned to introduce them. 'This is Senator Hooker, a good friend of Texas also.'

'Yeah?' drawled Tex, his eyes like gimlets boring into the uncomfortable senator. 'I know the senator. I bin tryin' fer two days ter contact him. He's sort of boss o' mine right now. Fact is, that's how I bumped into Jud this mornin'.'

His eyes didn't leave the senator's face.

'At the hotel they told me you were still out. Then the clerk said I was the second fellar to be enquirin' for you, senator, an' he pointed to a fellar sittin' waitin' at the bar. I recognised him as – Judson Cole.'

'Him?' Senator Hooker shot a startled glance at the body on the steps. 'But I don't know him. What did he want with me?' To Tex it seemed as though he was speaking the truth.

Regretfully the cowboy shook his head. 'He dived for my gun before I could ask him that question. He said he wanted to speak to you about your wallet, senator. You got no idea what he might have meant by that?'

The senator seemed to freeze as Tex went on, very quietly. 'That's what I came to tell you, senator. Jud an' his brother have got your wallet an' the papers you sent me after. Guess Lem's got them now, an' Lem's more intelligent than his brother. Why, I reckon Lem can even – read!' He shot the word out, and the paunchy senator seemed to reel back a step.

Tex abruptly finished with the senator. 'A few hours back I was goin' to tell you that I was through with that job you gave me. But now – hell and high furies won't stop me till I get my hands on them papers o' yourn, senator. Don't worry, I'll get 'em!'

But the senator, curiously, seemed most worried by the prospect. The dismay on his face was ludicrous, as he watched the big cowboy push through the throng that wanted him to stay and talk.

'Anything wrong, senator?' asked the old Governor anxiously.

'Wrong?' muttered Hooker. 'Not much there isn't!' and suddenly he turned and went quickly away round the back of the building.

Tex idled for a few moments at the top of the steps, feeling curiously depressed. He had done his bit in gaining the sympathy and support of the crowd for the Governor, and now it seemed that all the work was being left to others to perform.

He sat down to watch the activity in the square. Someone had removed the body of Judson Cole, the train-robber and renegade, so that wasn't there to remind him of the moment an hour ago when he had faced extinction – Jud, in a desperate gamble for his life, in the middle of answering a question, back of the hotel where the cowboy had grimly marched him, had suddenly clawed out at Tex's gun-hand. For a few seconds they had wrestled, Jud trying to turn the gun into Tex's face. Unexpectedly it had gone off, and Judson had slumped, dying without a word. But it had been a near thing; almost the train-robber had turned the tables on him.

Tex hadn't wanted him to die so quickly, so easily. The man was a renegade, and the cowboy had hoped to get useful information out of him before giving him his fair desserts. Jud had tried to bargain, had told a few names, and said that the Pancho raid was inspired by Yankee Americans with an eye to profit from war supplies. But he hadn't told Tex where he had come by the information, hadn't told him who was the big chief behind the trouble.

Yet Tex was pretty certain he knew, and that was making him sour now.

In the square the Rangers had set up tables and were organising the volunteers into parties. Only first-class, well-mounted horsemen were accepted. As Captain Gilray said, 'This is goin' to be mighty tough. I'd rather have five hundred tip-top men, than two thousand good, bad and indifferent ones. We'll have no time to nurse passengers on this trip.'

Tex suddenly felt proud as he saw what manner of men were coming forward to volunteer for special ranger work. They were the toughest men north of the Border; hard-riding, hard-shooting, hard-living men altogether – men who had lived near to death all their lives on this turbulent Border, and who had all too often brought leaden death to others. He felt proud, watching them, proud because he knew that he was responsible for this change of heart of theirs.

It was arranged that parties of ten should ride out, nine volunteers and one Ranger – and only the Ranger knew what the plan was. Dirk Humphrys was sent out to lead the first party; he and his men rode off to get their Winchesters, food and ammunition, and then cantered briskly through the square on their way out.

All the way the crowds lined the sidewalks, cheering the little party as they passed. A quarter of an hour later the second party went riding out, to the accompaniment of a further storm of cheering, and fifteen minutes later out rode Party No. 3.

As fast as they could be accepted and equipped, they were made up into parties and sent away. It was approaching mid-afternoon now, and the Rangers wanted to have a line stretching at least sixty miles along the Border by the following morning.

'I'm goin' to get five hundred good men, I can see,' said Captain Gilray in high humour. 'I want them between Pancho and the Border so that he can't escape us. Once an' for all, we've got to settle with that murderin' hombre!'

Then he saw Tex, sitting alone at the top of the steps, and he went up to speak with him. His eyes twinkled, looking at the big cowboy.

'Fer a man who's just scooped the pool,' said the

Ranger, dryly, 'you sure look mighty glum, Tex. How come? You all thinking that gal o' yours won't love you 'cause you blew that thar renegade's head off?'

'Naw, Alec,' said Tex, stretching uneasily. 'Guess from what I heerd from that gal, sendin' Jud ter kingdom come wouldn't get nothin' from her but a cheer. It ain't that, Alec. I got somep'n ter worry about.'

'It's not the same thing that got you so hoppin' mad, an hour back?' said Captain Gilray softly.

'Meanin'?'

'Meanin',' said the Ranger, 'you're a pretty even-tempered hombre normally, Tex. But when you came up on those steps, holy chuck-wagon, but you were mighty mad! I ain't never seen anyone quite so mad before. What was it burned you up so, Tex?'

Tex made little designs with the heel of his sandal in the dust by the side of the broad, shallow step. When he spoke his voice was bitter with murderous hatred. 'You gotta keep this quiet, Alec, because I've got no proof of what I am a-goin' to tell yer. Alec, I reckon I know who's behind all this Border trouble.'

'You do?' gasped the captain.

'Yeah, but at the moment it amounts only to a hunch. I won't say who he is – yet. He's a mighty big, powerful fellar, so strong I daren't say my piece until I've evidence enough to hang him afore any jury.'

'A politician, eh?'

'I ain't sayin', but he's the breed we don't care much for on the Frontier. An' d'you know why I'm mad, Alec? 'Cause I opine that the renegade's my boss.'

'You're workin' for him?' Captain Gilray's voice was incredulous.

'Up to a point. That point's reached just as soon as I lay hands on the evidence which seems able to scare the pants of him – reckon it should be enough to fit a collar round his fat neck – a rope collar.'

Tex wouldn't say any more at that. He went down to where the long queues of men waited patiently before the enlistment tables.

'I'm short o' Rangers,' Captain Gilray said, 'Will you lead a party, Tex? Reckon I couldn't get a finer fightin' man anywhere than you, an' you do know the plan, don't you?'

'Sure,' said Tex, brightening. 'Couldn't wish for better than to meet up with Pancho an' my old buddies, Lem an' the sidekick I winged.'

'Good. Wal, I won't be needin' you for another six hours, Tex, so grab some sleep. You'll ride out with a party that leaves around seven or eight tonight.'

Something in his tone made Tex ask the obvious question. 'Why am I goin' out just at that time, Alec?'

'Because,' said Gilray grimly, 'news has just come in that Pancho's operating in a territory twenty or thirty miles away. Guess he's so bold now he might even figger on comin' close to Lozier. So, Tex, I'm puttin' the pick of my men on that stretch of frontier ten to thirty miles out from Lozier, and you're one of them. If there's any fightin' to be done, Tex, I'm goin' to see that you're right there.'

'Thanks, pard,' said Tex with a grin. 'That just suits me fine an' dandy. I'll be back mighty soon – with my boots on!'

Tex knew he would be in the saddle most of the night, so wisely he took Gilray's advice and climbed on to his bed. Within five minutes he was fast asleep.

The sun was low over the western range when at last he stirred and finally swung his feet over the edge of the truckle bed. A yawn and a prodigious stretch and he felt suddenly wide enough awake for anything.

'Just get my stomach roun' some aigs an' bacon,' he thought, buckling on his guns, then he opened the door.

He slammed it, and it was the fastest thing he had ever done in his life; but even so he would have been sawn in half by the quartet of .45s but for the good luck that he had opened the door from a position to one side of it.

CHAPTER TEN

THE FINGER PROBES

That door hadn't started to move more than four or five inches, when the trigger-trained cowboy saw the gunmen silently waiting on the landing, four guns levelled at a region calculated to include a tall man's stomach.

He slammed it, instantly, and in the same movement went back and down on to the floor. Even as the door was shutting, even as he was falling, heavy, spinning, leaden death came smashing through the flimsy door, bursting in the panes, then continuing their murderous way into the bare little bedroom.

Even as he was falling, Tex's hands were drawing, finger squeezing as the sights came up ... bullets roaring away into the passage through the shattered door.

It all happened in a space of about two seconds. Tex felt the cloth tug on his right shoulder and that was all. But out in the passage he heard a scream, and then the firing ceased abruptly and heavy stumbling footsteps went crashing down the wooden stairs.

122

Tex didn't open the door until he was sure that two men had descended – he wasn't to be enticed out into any simple trap. When he went on to the stair head he saw blood on the wall, then a trail of blood leading down into the street. But of the men there was no sign; when he reached the sidewalk they had disappeared among the crowd.

He told Alec Gilray about the incident, his face grinning from ear to ear. 'Goldarn it,' he chuckled, 'I should've thought o' that. Reckon the big chief figgers I'm getting too good an idea of his business, an' he's all set on shovin' me 'cross the Great Divide.'

'You really think the inspirer of all this Border trouble set hired gunmen on to give you your chips, Tex?' The cowboy nodded casually. 'Wal, Tex, you ain't told me who he is, but I've put two an' two together. Ef anything happens to you, son, I'll take up the trail where you left off.'

'Thanks, Alec,' said Tex quietly. 'That's mighty broad o' you ter make that promise, an' I do appreciate it.' Between the big cowboy and the big Ranger a bond had sprung up in the last few hours. They were natural buddies from the moment they had set eyes on each other – like unto like ... stout-hearted fighting men both ...

Tex reached down and shook the captain's hand, then rammed his Winchester into the saddle-boot and cantered off to lead his men out through the town.

It was dark within a few miles, but they jogged steadily onwards, following a trail that was as well defined as a road, because of the passage of several hundred men before them. They rode easily, so as to conserve the energy of their horses, and by two in the morning they were approximately in the position where they had to halt until morning.

There was some confusion in the dark with parties catching up with each other, but when that happened the overtaking party halted for fifteen minutes before taking the trail again.

So it was, when dawn broke over the great Texas desert, that a line of armed men had sprung up between the Mexican marauders and the safety of their country. The swiftness of it all must have been disconcerting not only to Pancho, when he found out what had happened, but to small parties of emboldened Mexicans who were crossing the Border to try and join the raiders.

Tex's posse sighted one such party within a few minutes of light breaking. South of them, climbing from the bed of a dried-up watercourse, came a dozen swift-riding, nearly naked Mexicans. Tex immediately despatched a rider to warn the parties on either side of him that any firing they might hear as 'jes a li'l shootin' practice, an don't mean ter say we got our sights on Pancho.'

The Mexicans spotted them when they were about quarter of a mile away. Tex saw them pull back on their horses and send them rearing in confusion. 'Hold yore fire,' he ordered. 'Let's give them varmints a bit of encouragement,' and with that he turned tail and rode round the bare stone outcrop.

The Mexicans whooped with delight and came charging round after them. Eight Winchesters volleyed, then volleyed again. Six saddles lost their riders, one horse broke its neck through falling over a screaming Mexican, and that was enough for the survivors.

'Reckon that's not a bad bit o' work afore break-fast,' grinned Tex, when his other men came back, and coffee and the inevitable beans and bacon were prepared over a tiny fire that gave no betraying smoke. And then the party mounted, and on the stroke of six o'clock started due north from the frontier.

They didn't attempt to hide their progress, because on that broad desert it would have been attempting the impossible. As it was, whenever Tex and his party climbed above the normal level, as far as the eye could see, east and west of them, were puffs of dust cloud, marking the steady passage of the posses in their grim ride towards wherever the Mexican army was situated.

Because it was daylight, the posses were able to keep their distances from one another, so maintaining the long line up the Border. At times the posses were within hailing distance, and it would have been impossible for any mounted party to slip in between them.

All that morning they rode, hour after hour, under the blazing sun. The dust clung to their sweating faces and left them and their horses powdered from head to foot. Tex thought it was something of a ghostly army that was riding up that day from the Border, so white were they by the time they called the midday halt.

About four that afternoon, Tex saw a horseman detach himself from the posse east of his, and come riding headlong over. Instantly he stiffened. This looked like a message coming down the line.

It was. The horseman pulled up in a flurry of small stones and dust. 'Message fer you from down the line,' he reported to Tex. 'Last night Pancho raided a rancho less'n fifteen miles from Lozier. Guess he'll be pretty near into that thar place by now. Pass it on.'

With that he wheeled and raced back to join his own party, and Tex promptly despatched his fastest rider to relay the news to the posse west of him.

'He's gettin' near to Lozier,' said one of Tex's men. 'Mighty near.'

'Don't worry about Lozier,' said Tex. 'He won't go near the town, even though he's got several hundred fightin' men behind him. Lozier's too big, too well armed even though we're out hyar. No, what we must worry about are the ranchos an' villages that cain't pertect themselves like Lozier can.'

And in his heart he was adding to himself, 'Like the Two-by-Two.' He felt chilled, thinking of it. No one had ever expected the Mexican raiders to get so bold and come so close into Lozier, but here was news that the unexpected had happened.

Of course, Tex knew now why it was. It was deliberate, on the part of Pancho; it was a calculated act of brazen effrontery reckoned to rile the Texans and get them into reckless retaliation when he'd slipped away.

Tex thought, 'Guess we came out jes' in time. That raid last night, so near to Lozier, was his bluff bid, but he won't stay ter to see if it's called. Reckon the varmint thinks he's stirred up enough trouble, an' now he'll be raisin' hell fer the Border. Wish I was fifteen or twenty miles east o' hyar. I'd like ter get my sights on them galoots as they try'n break through our line ...'

Onward they rode, each man occupied with his

thoughts. And Tex's thoughts were of the laughing, quick-witted girl at the Two-by-Two ranch. Wondering if she were safe ... or if the ranch had been attacked and destroyed by the murderous raiders. Unconsciously he found himself kicking his horse into a gallop, as if he would ride down the perpetrators of such a deed.

Just before five in the afternoon, they heard what they had been waiting for. Suddenly a volley went up from the posse east of them, and when they turned in their saddles they saw hats waving excitedly.

'Pancho's been sighted somewhere down the line,' rapped Tex. 'Ready, fellars?'

They volleyed their Winchesters into the sky, then waved to the posse westwards, and in that way the message travelled from one posse to another.

Tex set spurs to his horse now, galloping eastwards but also slightly north of the nearest posse. In this way they hoped to encircle the Mexicans, and in fact that was what they did, eventually.

It was a posse under a Ranger named Jack Maitland who first sighted the Mexicans. Probably the raiders had seen their dust and were suspicious of these advancing, though widely separated, parties of horsemen. Probably Pancho who was no fool, instantly recognised it as an attempt to trap them, or at least intercept them if they tried to break through to the Border.

In an interval when the dust cleared, Pancho was able to see that the advancing posse consisted of only ten horsemen, and he guessed that the posses, two or three miles apart, comprised a like number.

His teeth flashed in a confident grin. 'Ten men

between us and the Border!' he ejaculated. 'Carramba, we will eat them!' But all the same the sight of those advancing posses convinced him that he had been long enough this side of the Border. It would be healthier for him and his men to cry enough and get over the Border before more serious attempts were made to trap them.

Pancho didn't see much significance in those small parties of advancing Texans. That was the biggest mistake he ever made.

He gave the order to his men to ride right through the nearest party. He thought it would be as easy as all that – one mad rush, maybe half a dozen or even a dozen of his men shot out of their high-pommelled saddles, then away in high spirits for the Border where they would be safe from pursuers ... And ten silent Texans lying in the desert with a hundred bullet holes through each of them.

Jack Maitland saw the movement when Pancho was about two miles away. You can't start four hundred horsemen into a gallop across the desert without raising a cloud of dust the size of a mountain. His men sent up a volley as a warning, but the posses east and west of him had seen the advancing Mexicans at almost the same second and didn't need telling.

Maitland saw that Pancho was heading directly for him and his men, so he gave the order to dismount and dig in – one man was detailed to lead the horses under cover, but he was back alongside the others before the first shot was fired. Maitland's men spread themselves on top of a short bluff, and went down behind the boulders that littered the top. When the howling, charging Mexicans were five or six hundred yards away, Maitland gave the order to fire. After that his men fired independently, as fast as they could load their smoking Winchesters.

The first volley emptied one or two saddles, but it brought down several horses and these caused unutterable confusion to the Mexicans pounding madly just behind. And the rapid fire that was maintained took further toll as the raiders came to closer range.

But that first volley did more than that – it brought panic into the heart of the Mexicans. They hadn't reckoned on the posse being equipped with these fine new repeating rifles that only the military up till now had possessed. It altered things; it's one thing to ride against men armed with revolvers with an effective range limited to about forty or fifty yards, but quite another when they're equipped with deadly, precision weapons that can kill even up to half a mile or more.

Instinctively Pancho pulled his horse round, and his mob swung after him. A minute later he recognised the mistake he had made and cursed himself for a fool. If he had kept on in the teeth of that murderous fire, perhaps forty or fifty of his men might have been shot down or lost their horses, but the main body would have crashed through unscathed.

As it was, Pancho and his Mexicans went wheeling out of range, and in that short time the neighbouring posses came hell for leather across the desert to join the Maitland party. Pancho lost the battle because of that fatal hesitation, though it amounted in the end to a mere matter of three or four minutes.

He saw the reinforcements converging from the

horizon, east and west of him, and his brain saw the danger in an instant. With a shout to his men, he sent his plunging Mexican pony straight for Maitland again.

Maitland calmly ordered 'Fire!' when they were nicely within range. Now thirty rifles blazed away, where before there were ten, and the carnage was terrible. The Mexicans didn't have a chance. For all the powder they burned, not a Texan was scratched. But then the Texans were dug in behind thick, sheltering rocks, and the Mexicans, with inferior, old-fashioned arms, were having to fire from the saddle.

This time the men aimed for the horses while they were at maximum distance, shifting to human targets as the galloping mob came closer.

Stricken horses went down, screaming, bringing other mounts down on top of them and breaking the solid front of the attacking force. Then the Winchesters opened their murderous, rapid fire on the Mexicans, and saddle after saddle was swept clean, long before the Mexicans were within eighty yards of the posses.

That last eighty yards was too much for the raiders; they hadn't the heart to take any further punishment from that screaming curtain of lead that spat out towards them. Suddenly they seemed to hesitate, no longer howling their war whoops, then the hesitation became a flight back out of range.

Maitland and the other posses ran for their horses at that. More posses were converging on the battle, and the Ranger knew that Pancho wouldn't attempt a third breakthrough in view of these reinforcements and the pasting he had just received.

One posse was left to round up the wounded

Mexicans and take them prisoners, and also to end the sufferings of the injured horses. The other two posses went loping off after the routed Mexicans.

About five minutes later yet another posse came galloping up, and at least another two could be seen racing towards them on either side. All the same Maitland, who had taken charge of the operations, knew that their strength was insufficient to make an open attack on the retreating mob of Mexicans, and he was content to follow steadily at a distance, pursuing, yet not overtaking.

That was all part of the Governor's plan. He wanted all the Mexicans to be captured or killed; and if Maitland had gone charging recklessly in, it would have left a breach in their line through which some of the enemy would certainly have escaped.

It must have unnerved the Mexicans. They were being pressed steadily backwards away from their own country, yet the visible force amounted to less than one-tenth of their number. But they knew it wasn't just Maitland's bunch they were up against – Maitland was merely a symbol of that far greater strength represented by those rapidly advancing clouds of dust that stretched into the blue distance east and west of him.

Pancho, so confident half an hour ago, so sure that he could outsmart the gringoes, all in one moment knew that he had over-reached himself – knew that this was the end for himself and his followers.

He was a bold man, and the situation made him desperate. When he had collected his force, and their horses had recovered from the last mad gallop, he turned suddenly in a headlong charge on Maitland's small party.

Maitland behaved as coolly as if he were back on the parade ground in Lozier.

A quiet word of command, and all dismounted. Two men led away the horses, while the rest quickly got down behind good cover. The third posse came galloping up at that moment, and then the posse which had been gathering in the prisoners sent six men flying in as reinforcements. Maitland took one look at the nearest posse, tearing in as if all the devils in hell were on their tails, and grinned.

'Reckon these hyar Mexes has left it too late,' he said grimly. 'Every minute that passes gives us more rifles agen 'em!'

That summed it up. If Pancho had crashed through against Maitland and his nine men in the first place, disregarding casualties, most of his party would now be heading for the safety of the border. But they had taken fright ... and had lost the day. Every minute from that first fight meant that the Texans' strength had grown. Against the superior fire-power of the Winchesters, and the tactics of the sharpshooters using them, the Mexicans stood little chance.

All the same, Maitland didn't take foolhardy risks. As soon as they were within effective range, he gave the order to fire. Again they aimed for the larger targets of the horses, when they were at maximum distance, shifting to human flesh nearer at hand.

It was sheer slaughter. It takes about half a minute for fast galloping horsemen to cover approximately a quarter of a mile. In that time thirty-six men can blaze off approximately three hundred rounds, and if they are good marksmen a majority will find targets at ranges up to five or six hundred yards, even fast-moving targets.

Pancho heard the hail of leaden hate screaming past him, saw horse after horse plunge head down into the sand, saw his once-proud little army turn to tatters long before they were anywhere near to the line of defenders ...

No one gave the order. Every Mexican knew that they hadn't a chance in hell of getting through those well-armed resolute defenders, so with one accord for the third time they turned and fled. And as they turned everyone knew it was the last charge they would make that day.

CHAPTER ELEVEN

TEX SETS 'EM ALIGHT

Pancho appeared to bear a charmed life – a stray bullet had clipped the flesh under his chin, but that was all. But he knew that this luck couldn't last much longer.

He took his men in headlong rout away from Maitland's party, at first not heeding where he was going until Lem Cole came riding alongside to say that they were heading for Lozier.

Lem wasn't feeling so good. He was wishing now that he had gone into Lozier to blackmail the senator, instead of sending his brother. But at the time it seemed riskier to go into town than it was to stay with the large and seemingly invincible raiding party.

Until half an hour ago, it had seemed the safest place in the world, in the midst of this bold, invading army. He had won his place by bluffing Pancho into believing that they were Senator Hooker's men, sent out to help them in their depredations. Lem had seen enough in the papers to understand why the senator was so anxious to get them back – they indicted Hooker as a man willing to trade in death so long as it helped his manufacturing concerns in Massachusetts to get war orders.

Pancho had believed his glib story after seeing one or two carefully-selected papers from the wallet, which indicated that Lem must be well in with the senator to have them in his possession.

Tucson Tommy was riding with him, his broken shoulder bandaged and strapped to his body. He was in great pain, and knew that if he didn't get medical attention he might go under. But where was he to get medical attention? And how? All he could do was cling, white-faced, to his bronc and follow where Lem led him.

Lem pushed his way to Pancho's side. He saw that the Mexican had momentarily lost control of the situation and of himself.

'Hey,' he shouted. 'Where'n the heck d'yer think you're goin'? You ain't aimin' ter hit Lozier, air you?

Pancho pulled round at that, circling northwards.

Half a mile behind, the blasted gringoes pulled round, too. Now several more posses had added themselves to Maitland's bunch, so that a solid force of seventy or eighty well-armed cowboys were on his trail. And still other posses were galloping up across the cactus-littered desert.

Lem had noticed something that Pancho had missed. Those clouds of dust that betokened distant fast-moving posses were not only closer together, but towards the horizon they were advancing in front of the retreating Mexicans. Lem swore as he saw and understood, and that cussword was a mighty good compliment to the Governor's long-range planning.

The plan had worked in every detail, and now the 'finger' was beginning to probe the life out of the raiders.

Lem pointed out the significance of those advancing parties on the horizon. 'Get it, Pancho?' he gasped. 'Them parties is goin' to swing round an' meet north of us. Then we'll be plumb in the middle of a circle of Texans armed with Winchesters. I calkilate we'll last ten minutes when that happens.'

Pancho understood, and his swarthy face was worried.

'Madre de dios!' he whispered. 'You, Lem, tell me what I do!'

Lem said, bluntly, 'Our on'y chance is ter hold 'em up until dark. The moon don't rise fer two-three hours, and I reckon our best bet is to try an' sneak through their lines while it's at its blackest. Reckon most o' yore men will go under at that, but it gives a few of us a chance ter make the Border. You willin' ter risk it?'

'Sure,' nodded Pancho emphatically. 'Guess I sweeng ef them Rangers catch me. You come, Lem?'

'Reckon I sweeng, too, otherwise,' mimicked Lem, and that was a good enough answer for the Mexican chief. Whatever the risk, the renegades had to take it.

Shortly after this they topped a bluff and looked down upon a pretty large ranch. Lem pulled up and pointed. 'Pancho,' he said, 'see them thick mud walls, an' that high compound? Reckon with the two or three hundred men we've still got, we c'n hold that until dark.'

Pancho nodded. Now, suddenly, he was himself again, his brain scheming for any advantage, desperately planning to overturn the tables on the advancing Texans. In an instant he saw the possibilities of that solidly built rancho, and at once he turned, rapping out orders to his men.

'Fernandez,' he ordered a lieutenant. 'You take fifty men with good rifles and fight a delaying action against these gringoes. You've got to hold them back as long as possible, retreating on the rancho as slowly as you can.'

He saw the men dismount and take cover on the rocky escarpment, then gathering their horses Pancho led his men in a swift charge on the ranch buildings.

There was some resistance, because they had been spotted on the skyline, but the situation was desperate and Pancho sent his men riding in regardless of casualties. The dozen defenders were overwhelmed within minutes, and were either killed outright or taken prisoner.

So it was that when Tex McQuade came riding in for the kill, shortly before dusk, it was to find the Mexican army holed up in a ranch called ... Two-by-Two.

All the posse leaders had been summoned to a meeting by Captain Gilray, on top of the bluff which had been cleared of the Mexican rearguard. The Ranger explained the situation. 'We've driven all the Mexes under cover of the rancho, but I don't reckon they'll stay there much more than another hour. They're in a desperate situation, completely surrounded, an' I guess they'll make a break for it as soon as it's dark. The moon doesn't rise for two or three hours tonight, and that should give them ample time to sneak out.

'By then we should have two to three hundred men surrounding the rancho, with more coming in every few minutes. But that ain't many now that we're spread out in a circle round them – I reckon our line's at least three miles long, an' that means we've only got one man every twenty yards or more. And that ain't much, considerin' it'll be as dark as the inside of a cow's belly from eight until eleven.'

Someone said, 'Yeah, an' Winchesters ain't much good in the dark.'

'No,' said Alec Gilray. 'If we have any action in the dark, you'd better stick to your six-shooters. It'll be close work, all the time.'

'Think we can hold 'em?' asked someone bluntly, and at that the Ranger Captain shook his head regretfully.

'Not now it's dark. If I were Pancho I'd just wait until it was at its blackest, then I'd split my men into half a dozen parties an' tell 'em to ride hell for leather in different directions at our line. We'd never even see 'em until they were on top of us, an' that way I guess most o' the varmints would get away.'

That quietened them. So far the plan had worked out well. The trouble was that they had met up with the Mexicans too late in the afternoon to get sufficient force together to ride in and wipe them out. And that meant that the advancing darkness was threatening to outwit them, after all their planning and hard-riding.

Tex was rolling a smoke, lying on his stomach, his eyes narrowed to where the ranch lay in the fading light. Suddenly he hurled the unlighted cigarette to the ground and stood up.

'Captain,' he said, 'I don't reckon ter sit on my

138

fanny an' watch them thievin', murderin' Mexes lick us after all. I'm a'goin' ter do something about it.'

Gilray's eyes glinted with humour as he looked up at the big, rough cowboy with the battered, cheerful face. 'Something?' he repeated. 'But what?' and that floored Tex.

He stood there and scratched his head and then admitted, 'Don't rightly know, Captain. But I guess I'll take a walk over to the rancho an' see ef I c'n think o' somethin'. A walk would do me good, anyway.'

Nobody saw him walk across, but all the same he reached the ranch buildings. It took him half an hour, and it tore every button off his shirt in the process, but at length, unobserved by the defenders, he came on his belly under a fence and into the cover of a big barn.

By this time it was pitch black dark, and Gilray was standing-to with his men, ready to shoot down the charge, if it were at all possible. In the distance, behind the compound wall, they could hear the jingling of harness metal and they knew that the Mexicans were mounting and preparing to run the gauntlet.

Suddenly one Ranger called, 'Alec, what's that?'

Everyone turned. From the direction of the rancho a huge flame shot up; within seconds there was a roar like a blast furnace and fiery tongues went leaping into the night sky. One minute there was darkness everywhere; the next this enormous fire lighted up the rancho and its near vicinity almost as if it were daylight.

And five minutes later another barn started to go up in flames on the opposite side of the rancho.

Gilray chuckled admiringly. 'That,' he remarked

proudly, 'is the work of our fightin' cowboy, Mister McQuade. Guess he did think o' somep'n after all!'

There were shouts of dismay from the Mexicans, and some went and tried unavailingly to put out the betraying flames.

For while those barns raged and burned they were virtually trapped within the compound; Tex had eliminated the advantage that the darkness had given them. If they tried to escape, no longer could they do so secretly; now they would have to ride out openly, and they would be targets all the way for an enemy who would close in on them as they dashed up.

Tex, a sombrero on his head (the late owner had somehow contracted a broken neck), was boldly riding around in the middle of the panicky bewildered Mexicans. Pancho was sending out search parties to try and hunt down the enemy in their midst, and Tex found himself being detailed to follow one of them. In this way he found time to set fire to a third stack of hay.

But Tex wasn't riding around just for the hell of it; this was the Two-by-Two ranch, and a girl he knew had invited him to call on her there, and he reckoned, being so near, it would be nice an' polite if he did so now.

After a while he spotted guards on a 'dobe building that seemed to have been used as a store – it had small windows with bars across and a particularly formidable door. Just the sort of place where you would put prisoners. The pair of high-hatted Mexican guards, dolefully watching the raging fires, appeared to hold the prisoners without much attention from themselves.

Tex quietly slid round to the back and pulled himself up to the small, barred window. A single oil lamp cast a yellow glow on the occupants.

They were five in number – four men and a girl. Two of the men were bandaged and a third was lying in a corner on some sacks as if seriously hurt. As Tex peered in, the girl was bending over the recumbent man, attending to him carefully.

Tex called quietly, 'Oh, Lavender!' She turned, her face startled, then lighting up joyfully. A face suddenly turned happy in that warm lamplight. She ran to the window where Tex grinned down on her.

'Tex!' she called softly, incredulously.

'Me,' he agreed. 'An' now what you got ter say about my plug ugly face, Lavender?'

She smiled up at him. 'Never,' she declared, 'have I seen a face so welcome, cowboy!'

Tex grinned and then turned to the man who was standing behind Lavender. The bandage on the old man's head hid his features, but Tex guessed that it was the father he had seen for a few seconds down at Lozier station one time.

'Reckon, Mr Grey, I should tell you that I'm the galoot responsible fer setting fire ter them barns o' yores.'

'You did?'

'Sure,' said Tex, and then explained calmly. 'Thought I'd better tell yer, Mr Grey, 'cause I'm aimin' ter take yore daughter away from you, if she'll have me.'

The old man looked at the girl, then said simply, 'Looks like she'll have you, cowboy. Reckon she's been set on you fer sometime, an' when Lavender gets a wish in her head, there ain't no stoppin' her till she gets what she's after. Reckon you'll regret this day, son!'

'Father!' exclaimed Lavender, shocked, but the old man just grinned at Tex through the bars.

Tex decided he'd been there long enough. At any moment the sentries might decide to walk round the store hut and then he would be spotted and even if he shot them down it would betray his presence to the other Mexicans.

He said, softly, 'Keep smilin' everyone. I'll be back fer you. Take this pistol o' the Mex that I knocked down a while back. But don't use it until you have to. So long!'

With that he disappeared soundlessly.

Lights were blazing in the ranch house, and as Tex slipped across between the shadowy buildings he saw Lem and Pancho fling themselves from their horses and enter the building. The cowboy crept round until he discovered a window looking in on them.

Tucson had found a bottle of whiskey and was sitting huddled over it, pain-wracked and near the end of his tether.

Lem alone seemed less disturbed – perhaps because he had lived a life always so near to the hangman's noose that he was used to ticklish situations. He reached across and took the bottle from Tucson.

'You've had enough,' he growled. 'Rate yore goin' on, you'll never be able to sit yer cayuse, Tuc.' He took a drink, and it went down as easily as if it were water, raw though it was.

'That blasted fire sure put paid to our chances o' breakin' through,' he growled.

'Madre mia!' was all the Mexican could say.

Lem took another swig from the bottle, his eyes narrowed in thought. His brain was racing desperately, seeking some way out of this jam. And suddenly his knuckles whitened as his fingers gripped hard on to the bottle; he sat up straight, his eyes blazing with triumph.

'Got it!' he exclaimed. The others turned quickly toward him, hope in their eyes.

'You got plan – idea?' queried Pancho.

'Yeah, I got an idea,' said Lem, nodding his head slowly. He was still thinking out the details.

'Reckon we c'n escape?' asked Tucson, eagerly. 'I gotta get outa hyar quick, Lem, gotta get a doctor!'

He didn't notice the contemptuous look that his leader gave him. Tucson wouldn't need a doctor if these Texans captured them, and he couldn't see the wounded Tucson sitting a saddle long enough to outride the cowboys once they got on to his trial. And that was provided his plan worked out right. Still, he'd take Tucson along, if only to use him to fool pursuers after they'd got through.

'Thees idea, caballero?' began the Mexican with a flattering smile. 'How can you make all my men escape?'

'No can do,' grunted Lem. 'I c'n see a way of us escaping – you, Pancho, me an' Tucson. But no more than that.'

'But my men?' began Pancho. 'What weel happen to them?'

Lem just shrugged. 'They'll have ter get their own ideas,' he said callously. 'This plan will work for a few, but not for all yore durned army, Pancho. Now, listen.'

143

Tex strained his ears at the window, but all the same missed the beginning of what Lem was saying. Then the train-robber raised his voice, and Tex was able to hear.

'... a cinch ... Texans ain't like you Greasers ... they got an unholy respec' fer wimmin. We gotta take advantage o' this hyar chivalrous streak. Pancho, we three'll ride out ter where them prisoners is. We'll get the gal an' ride out towards them Texans without lettin' on to anyone what we intend ter do.'

Pancho said something which Tex didn't catch, and Lem answered with brutal directness.

'Ef you tell yore men what we're plannin' ter do, they'll all want ter come with us, an' I reckon that wouldn't be so handy when it comes to bargainin' with them Rangers. An' when you tell 'em they can't come, what d'yer think they'll do? Think they'll sit quietly an' watch their chief ride out on 'em, leaving 'em to a pretty sure death sentence hyar? Nope, Pancho; ef you air comin', you gotta fergit yore *hombres* – they'll have ter look after themselves.'

Pancho made up his mind. 'I come,' he said promptly. Men such as Pancho don't bother much about other men's skins when their own is in danger of being dug open by flying .45 shells.

Lem rose. 'Thar's plenty hosses at the rail. You, Tucson, lead a spare fer the gal. An' remember, when we ride across that firelit patch, we gotta make sure that the Texans see thar's a gal with us, otherwise they'll jes' open fire an' shoot us all down.'

'And when we get to thees Rangers?' queried Pancho.

'Jes' leave it all ter me,' Lem told them. 'I'll be

144

ridin' with my gun in the gal's ribs, an' if there's any fancy tricks I reckon ter blow her purty waist through an' through. Ef we get out, she'll go out afore us,' he said grimly.

Tex stiffened in horror. With men as desperate as these, anything could happen to Lavender Grey.

Lem paused while the other two took a swig from the nearly empty bottle, then he finished it off himself. He seemed quite cheerful now.

'I guess this is one more time that I'm a-goin' ter put one across them pesky Rangers,' he chuckled. 'They won't lay a hand on us ef they're sure that by doin' so the gal will get hers. C'mon, let's go.'

CHAPTER TWELVE

RETRIBUTION FOR A RAT

Lem paused on the ranch-house steps. It was a curious scene that met his eyes. Everywhere Mexicans sat their restive mounts behind the cover of the high 'dobe wall – three hundred helpless men.

Beyond them, from three points, red flames towered skywards, showering sparks and flaming masses of hay high into the star-lit sky, lighting up the place almost as if it were midday and not ten at night.

Not a shot was being fired, by the attackers or by the Mexicans; for all the raiders knew they might have been alone on the ranch. But Lem wasn't deceived; he knew that a thin line of well-armed men lay crouching in the shadows beyond the red circle of light, their guns ready to spit death if the Mexicans ventured from cover.

Pancho stood by his side, watching for a minute or so. Tucson seemed slow, so Lem called, without turning, 'C'mon Tuc. That thar bottle's empty.'

'Yeah,' growled the voice of Tucson, and then all three swung up on their horses and Lem led the way across the crowded compound to where the small prison hut stood. As they came clear of the mounted Mexicans, one spoke rapidly to Pancho, who replied quickly in turn.

'What's he say?' asked Lem suspiciously.

'He want to know where we go,' explained Pancho.

'An' you said?'

'I tell heem we try a treek to save them all. We goin' out to barter prisoners' lives for our own.'

'Good,' approved Lem. 'Now, that was real smart-thinkin' on yore part, Pancho. Reckon I c'n see why they made you chief o' yore mob, now.'

At the hut Lem and Pancho dismounted. 'Get them trabajadores ter fetch the gal outa the cala-boose,' ordered Lem and Pancho translated the order to the sentries.

At the last minute it seemed as though the men inside the hut tried to drag her back to them, but one of the sentries quickly swung the butt of his rifle and while they stepped back out of range the other pulled Lavender out into the firelit compound and then slammed the door.

Lem promptly jabbed the six-shooter into the pit of the girl's stomach. 'Ma'am,' he said with brittle politeness, 'I don't wish ter do you no harm, but I reckon all the same ter blow you inter li'l pieces ef you try'n escape, sabe?'

'Sabe,' said the girl promptly, looking beyond him.

'Now mount,' Lem ordered, indicating the led horse, and Lavender, regardless of her thin dress, swung up easily astride the pony. Lem mounted and closed in on her, gun never wavering from her slim straight back.

They rode out at that, past the whispering, mounted Mexicans – Lavender between the Mexican and the Texan, with the fourth horseman tailing close in the rear.

Boldly Lem set their horses for the brush that marked the line of light from the still-roaring fires. Nothing happened as they cantered forward, not a shot came their way – there was not a sound from the surrounding darkness.

Lem kept grimly on, knowing full well that the Texan sharpshooters must have recognised that a girl was in the middle of the party, because of the strong light that came from behind the crowded compound to where the small prison hut stood.

They were a couple of hundred yards from the compound when a shout came to their ears.

'Halt, thar! Who are you, an' where d'yer think you're goin'?'

Lem spoke brazenly, not bothering to hide the truth.

'Me,' he said, 'guess I'm one o' the hombres you're out ter get yore mits on. On'y I reckon ter disappoint yer. See this gal hyar? Wal, I got a gun in her back.' There was a gasp from Lavender as the hard steel jabbed viciously into her unprotected body. Lem's voice rose to a brutal roar, and when they heard it the men in the shadows knew that he meant every word that he said.

'Ef anyone o' you tries ter jump us,' rasped Lem, 'my trigger finger'll do somep'n ter this hyar gun. That'll be curtains fer this young lady. I ain't kiddin', I'll blow her ter smithereens ef anyone so much as moves a foot towards us. You understand?'

'I understand,' said the voice from the dark. 'But what do you perpose ter do, *hombre*?'

'I perposeter ride nice an' steady like past you, right as far as the Border,' said Lem calmly. 'I'm takin' the gal all the way so as to make sure that thar ain't no tricks played on us.'

'An' the girl? What'll you do with her when you get to the Border?'

'Aw, mebbe let her go free,' said Lem contemptuously. 'I ain't one fer wimmin.'

The voice persisted from the darkness, probably playing for time in the hope that something might turn up to disrupt the Border bandit's bold escape plan. 'What guarantee have we that if we let you go free you'll keep yore word an' let the gal loose at the Border.'

Lem, contemptuous, spat into the firelit sand. 'You ain't got no guarantee,' he said coldly. 'An' I ain't givin' none. I don't need ter. I got the whip hand, an' I know it. What's more, you know it. You jes' gotta take a chance on savin' this gal's life – by doin' nothin'.'

Lem didn't even wait for approval from the hidden Rangers. 'Gid up,' he said, and sent his mount trotting along the southward trail.

From the shadows the Texans watched – the two men riding close up to the girl, the renegade's gun pressed into her ribs, and behind the bandaged figure of the third man, drooping with pain.

They saw them ride up, so that the party was level with the nearest snarling, cursing, finger-twitching Texan. They saw the party level with them, then passing though ... with no one now between them and the Border.

And then the bandaged man spurred swiftly up and dived across Lem's horse, his crooked arm dragging the startled raider with him.

Pancho wheeled, then jabbed rowel spurs viciously into the side of his mount. The horse screamed with the pain of it and took to a gallop. Fifty rifles spoke as one, and horse and rider went down in a heap that never moved a muscle after hitting earth.

It was the end of Pancho the Mexican, Border raider and trouble-maker.

Lem's gun went off in mid-air, but if it hit anything it was the planet Venus. Then as they crashed on to the ground, Tex wrestled the gun from his opponent's hand and tossed it away.

Lem came painfully on to his knees to find himself faced by the crouching Tex McQuade, two blue bores staring like sightless eyes at him.

Tex rapped, 'Ditch yore other gun, *hombre.*' Slowly the train-robber did as he was ordered. Rangers ran up at that moment to grab the renegade, but Tex waved them off.

His voice was like the raw note of a file tearing through plate steel. 'I got somep'n ter settle with this *hombre,*' he said. 'He left me tied ter die at the hands o' Pancho an' the gang, way back in the desert. He beat me up an' kicked me unconscious before that – still while I was tied. I seen this fellar do the dirtiest of tricks, an' I aim to let him know what sufferin's like before he passes out.

'I killed yore brother, Lem!' The bandit started at that. 'But I regret that he went out without much pain. Guess you'll have to take his share right now.'

Tex unbuckled his gun belt and handed it to Lavender who had come to his side. 'Hold that, honey,' he said, 'I'll be comin' back to you soon.'

Lavender knew that nothing could keep him from that act of retribution, and wisely she didn't try to stay him. 'Good luck, Tex,' she said, and then, as he went forward, 'Ride him, cowboy!'

They fought on the edge of the desert by the glow of those flaming barns and the stack of hay. A circle of men marked the perimeter of the 'ring' – there were no ropes, no referee, no rounds ... and within seconds Tex knew there were no rules either.

They came together, grappling in the middle of the ring, their feet scuffling in the sand. Lem was a big man and strong, if anything heavier than the cowboy. Tex tried to throw him, but his feet went from under him and instead he fell backwards. Lem lifted his boot and without hesitation kicked the cowboy in his face.

Tex went reeling back, and his opponent was on to him in a minute. Fists toughened by years of hard-living in the open range and the back hills, Lem smashed into the stumbling, uncertain cowboy. Left-right, left-right, left ... Blood fountained from Tex's face, and again he went down in the sand.

Like lightning Lem kicked again, and again Tex took the blow on his head. Then Lem was into his body, wading in with his feet, kicking it to break the ribs of the cowboy.

But the ex-fighter was tough. He was rolling all the time, to try and soften the blows, and he was succeeding better than the onlookers thought. Rolling and seeking to get on his feet again, and give vent to the murder that was in his heart.

This was the second of the gang that he had met in a stand-up fight, and both had resorted to dirty work from the beginning. And the advantage is always with the man that gets in with the first foul blow.

Another lunging kick sent Tex's head snapping back. It looked bad, looked as if he had got his chips.

Then a flying form hurtled into the shambling bulk that was the murderous Lem, hands tore and scratched at him in an effort to save the cowboy from being kicked to death. Looking up, Tex saw that it was Lavender Grey, coming to his rescue.

In an instant fifty men were on to the train-robber, holding him back. One big Ranger spoke for them all: 'You're a dirty, low-down fighter, Renegade. I guess we'll jes' string you an' have done with it. What say, fellars?'

'Aye!' they called, and the roar was low and guttural; it came from the throats of men who hated and who wanted to destroy the object of their hatred.

Only one man was against it. He came staggering up from the sand, wiping the blood from his streaming face with his sleeve.

'You ain't goin' ter string no one up,' Tex said. 'Not until I've finished with this *hombre*. Get back an' leave him ter me. Now I know how he fights I'll be able ter take care o' him, see ef I don't.'

There was some muttering and shaking of heads, and Lavender began to plead with Tex. He looked bad, and the red light from the flaming barns didn't improve appearances. But Tex shoved the girl to one side, gently, saying, 'I'll take care o' him, Lavender. I ain't done yet. Thanks fer comin' to my rescue, gal,

152

but – don't do it again!'

Lem came in sneering. He thought he had his opponent groggy, and he still had a trick or two up his sleeve. Two yards from the waiting Tex he took a swift jump forward and lashed out yet again with his ponderous foot. It was aimed to smash Tex's kneecap, and by rights it should have put the cowboy down once again – down at the renegade's brutal feet.

But somehow it didn't connect. Tex hadn't trained in the ring for nothing. He swayed slightly on his feet, and Lem's foot swung wide of the mark. Tex promptly dropped flat on the outstretched leg, and Lem's scream rose to heaven.

The cowboy's quick manoeuvre had sent the bandit into the 'splits', and when you are not used to it, and over a hundred and eighty pounds of steel-hard brawn and muscle crashes down on to the extended limb, it – hurts.

Lem rolled over in agony, torn muscles searing him like a fire along the inside of his leg. Tex staggered to his feet and stood over his opponent. One foot was drawn back to smash in the ribs of the helpless bandit. And then he walked away.

If he couldn't lick the sonofagun without resorting to dirty tactics, then he'd pack up as a fighter.

The crowd didn't understand. 'Go in, Tex!' they hollered. 'Kick the livin' daylights out of the so-and-so!'

But Tex only shook his head and stood back in the fireglow until his opponent had recovered sufficiently to be able to stand erect again.

Then Tex waded in.

It wasn't one-sided. Lem still had his great

strength and so far had suffered less mauling than his opponent. And at all times he was prepared to pull off a dirty, unexpected trick.

But the big cowboy walked in as if he couldn't feel the smashing fists that came back at him. He fought him like the boxer he was, with fists clenched and hurting, every blow telling and bringing gasps of pain from the bandit.

He tore into his opponent regardless of the dirty tricks that the fellar might try to pull off. In he came, always in, never retreating. His arms pumped in and out like pistons, seeming intent on trying to smash the bandit down by sheer force of his pounding fists.

Round and round the ring of cheering men they went, and then the renegade fell.

Tex stood back and gave him plenty of time to recover. He even let him stand for half a minute before moving in once more. And then the punishment started all over again. This time Lem wasn't long on his feet. The shattering blows that tore through his guard jolted his head unmercifully, and left him so dazed he was hardly able to swing a fist in return. Down he went a second time, and again Tex stood back and gave him full time to recover. Lem came up slowly. Tex smashed him back into the sand with a couple of cruel right hooks that nearly tore the ear off the renegade.

Panting, Lem looked up from the sand, and saw his implacable enemy coldly waiting for him to rise again. And now he understood. Tex was going to stand back and give him chance to fight whilst there was an ounce of strength left in his body. Tex intended to knock the last bit of fight out of him for all the rottenness and treachery that he had perpetrated on others.

'He wants to get me on my knees, sobbin' fer mercy,' snarled Lem through bloodied lips. 'Wal, he'll have a long time ter wait.' He was no craven, this bandit; he wasn't going to give in even though he knew he hadn't a chance now of beating the cowboy.

He stood swaying, then somehow found strength to walk into the cowboy, fists battering in a final spasm of murderous hatred. 'I'll kill yer yet,' he sobbed through his bleeding mouth.

Tex didn't retreat a step. He took everything that came, and then relentlessly marched forward, hammering the sense out of his rascally opponent.

Lem went down. It took him a couple of minutes this time to get to his feet, and now the ring of men was silent, wondering when it would end. Tex smashed him down twice more, and now, at last, terror came into the train-bandit's black heart – a terror no less than that which he had inspired into many another man's heart before.

It was the moment Tex was waiting for. He heard the renegade begin to sob and moan for mercy, for an end to be put to this thrashing – for anything, even a bullet, which would permit him to escape further pain. Tex quit then; he felt he had avenged himself and others.

He was turning away when a shrill warning shout broke from a point way up east of then … a shout, and then a solitary rifle erupted with its sharp, whip-like crack.

Everyone spun round. 'The Mexes!' someone shouted. 'They're making a dash fer it!'

They were. They had seen their chief ride away,

and they suspected a double-cross because he didn't come back. Fernandez swore mightily and said he'd hunt Pancho down if it was the last thing he ever did. Then he vaulted on to his horse, and the rest of the Mexicans did the same – they went tearing across the soft, fire-lit sand right on the tracks of their late leader. Because of the interest in the fight, the Mexicans were half-way towards the brush before a lone sentry spotted them.

They were too near for rifle fire from the bunch around the fighters. 'Fan out!' yelled a burly Ranger, and at that the Texans leapt forward in an extending line to meet the charging enemy. It was a duel between mounted men and a small number on foot, but the Texans again had better weapons in their slick six-shooters, and their aim wasn't handicapped by bucking broncs. In came the Mexicans, screaming defiance at the top of their voices. A stream of lead hit them at forty yards out, and the screams changed to groans and shrieks of pain. Horses went mad and lashed out and ran amok down the line of Mexicans, and men were thrown and were trampled to death by the later horsemen. For a few seconds it looked like some witches' cauldron boiling over as men and horses tumbled and fell and brought others tumbling and falling atop of them.

Tex took one look at his opponent. But he saw that Lem was safe – he had no strength left now for a getaway; he lay stretched face downwards in the sand, blood saturating the earth by his head.

Lavender had come to his side, and Tex put his arm protectingly around her. In the crimson fire-light that still lit the horizon for miles around on the open desert, the carnage looked ghastly. Then the fight seemed to boil over and encompass the two standing there.

Tex shouted, 'Keep right back o' me, Lavender!' and when a Mexican came hurtling through, trying to charge them down, Tex jumped for the horse's head, clung for a brief second, then sent it over on to its side in a smooth steer throw. Tex had no guns, and that Mexican passed quietly out of the ruckus with a large fist under his chin.

The cowboy swung over, kneed the scared pony across to where Lavender was standing on the fringe of the battle, and picked her up just as a mob of Mexes broke through. A second later and she would have been under their hooves.

Tired, Tex pulled his horse away from the fight. On the edge of the bluff he pulled up and looked back. 'Guess they don't need me,' he opined. 'Some of the Mexes'll get through, but not many. Reckon most of that raiding force will be wrapped around lead pellets within another five minutes. Now you an' I will go an' see that dad o' yourn. He'll be anxious ter see yer, I reckon. Tomorrow—'

'Tomorrow?' she repeated, watching his bruised and bleeding face as he held her close to him.

'Tomorrow Captain Gilray will find the papers on that varmint, Lem. Reckon the evidence there will guarantee a place on the same cottonwood tree as the renegade for Mister Senator Claude C. Hooker.'

It did. But Tex didn't bother to go and see the stringing up. He was busy planning new barns with the old man who was shortly to become his father-in-law.